Hermes rolled his eyes. "Okay, enough! Now, instructions first, questions afterward. I could be all godlike and get a little flowery but that would get us nowhere fast, and since you all need to get somewhere fast, I'll put it to you straight. You're going back in time. Here's the rule: don't change anything in the past or it will alter the future. Seriously. And it might not be good. Any questions?"

"Uh, yes," Iole said, thinking fast, as the others just looked at one another, confused. "How far back are we going?"

"Roughly thirteen centuries. Next?"

"Lust is . . . is . . . back in time?" Pandy asked.

MYTHIC MISADVENTURES
BY CAROLYN HENNESY

Pandora Gets Jealous
Pandora Gets Vain
Pandora Gets Lazy
Pandora Gets Heart
Pandora Gets Angry

PANDORA

Gets Heart

BOOK IV

CAROLYN HENNESY

BLOOMSBURY

NEW YORK BERLIN LONDON SYDNEY

First published in the United States of America in January 2010
by Bloomsbury Books for Young Readers
Paperback edition published in January 2011
www.bloomsburykids.com

For information about permission to reproduce selections from this book, write to
Permissions, Bloomsbury BFYR, 175 Fifth Avenue, New York, New York 10010

The Library of Congress has cataloged the hardcover edition as follows:
Hennesy, Carolyn.
Pandora gets heart / by Carolyn Hennesy.—1st U.S. ed.
        p.   cm.
Summary: Pandy, Alcie, Iole, and Homer face many dangers as they make their
way to the sacred Mount Ida in Phrygia to capture another deadly evil—lust.
ISBN: 978-1-59990-439-9 (hardcover)
1. Pandora (Greek mythology)—Juvenile fiction. [1. Pandora (Greek mythology)—Fiction.
2. Mythology, Greek—Fiction. 3. Gods, Greek—Fiction. 4. Goddesses, Greek—Fiction.
5. Adventure and adventurers—Fiction.] I. Title.
PZ7.H3917Pah 2010   [Fic]—dc22   2009022664

ISBN: 978-1-59990-595-2 (paperback)

Typeset by Westchester Book Composition
Printed in the U.S.A. by Quad/Graphics, Fairfield, Pennsylvania
2 4 6 8 10 9 7 5 3 1

All papers used by Bloomsbury Publishing, Inc., are natural, recyclable products
made from wood grown in well-managed forests. The manufacturing processes
conform to the environmental regulations of the country of origin.

For Donald
Anar

PANDORA
Gets Heart

CHAPTER ONE
The Ruse

Iole was moving on tiptoe.

She'd heard giggling from the cabin. And an occasional high-pitched shriek. Which meant they were in there . . . laughing about something. What? Her? *At* her? How they had completely overlooked her? Forgotten all about . . .

In the girls' cabin, aboard the ship bound for Thessaly, Pandy and Alcie were clutching their sides with glee, wiping tears from their eyes and slapping the air (and each other) playfully.

In the corridor, Iole crept to the cabin door, her ear pressed against the wood. She caught single words, bits of sentences.

". . . never . . ."

". . . obvious . . ."

". . . we'll have fun . . ."

Just then the ship leaned hard to one side and Iole was slammed up against the door.

"Ooooff," she cried, then quickly covered her mouth.

Instantly, the sounds inside the cabin stopped. As she was backing down the corridor, she thought she heard a "shhh" but couldn't be sure. About five meters away, she began singing loudly, walking toward the cabin again. Opening the door, she found Alcie sitting on the end of her cot, brushing her red hair, and Pandy, on the floor, playing with the enchanted rope Athena had given to her. Both girls looked supremely calm.

"Hey, Alcie," Pandy said, not immediately looking up, "how small do you think this rope could get without disappearing entirely? . . . Oh, hi, Iole."

"Hi," she said, still standing in the doorway.

"Hey, Iole," Alcie said. "Wow, were you gone?"

"Yes," she said flatly. "I went up on deck to take a last look at Crete in the distance."

"Oh?" said Alcie.

"Yes, Alcie. It was my home, as you know."

"Yep."

"The place of my birth . . . a number of years ago."

"Right. Got it."

"A certain number of years."

"Hey, Alcie," Pandy said, pinching the skin on top of her thumb to keep from laughing, "speaking of home, what's the first thing you're gonna do when we get back?"

Iole wondered if they were ignoring her on purpose. She slowly started to clench her hands.

"Oh, lemon rinds, after I write to Homer? I'm going to go find the biggest, most beautiful, most expensive girdle and make my dad buy it for me as a present."

"Present?" Iole said, perking up.

"Uh . . . uh . . . that's great," Pandy said. "I think I'm going to spend a lot of time playing with my baby brother. Of course, he won't be such a baby anymore . . . maybe he even had another birth-day . . . gosh, I don't know."

"Mmmm, maybe," said Alcie. "They grow up so fast."

Now, turning her head away, Iole was getting angry.

She knew that neither of her best friends had her superior brain power (not even combined could they match her) and that getting them to, just once, remember something *this* important on their own was next to impossible, but that's why she'd left clues for the past three days. She had casually whistled the tune to "Happy Maiden Day to You," talked about her fifth birth-day party as they sailed past Crete, and even mentioned what her favorite present had been that day—a signed first edition of Plato's *The Republic*. ("At the age of five?" Pandy had asked incredulously. "Naturally," Iole replied.)

Lots of clues. Soooo many clues . . .

But nothing.

She willed herself to relax her tightly curled fists and turned, smiling, back to Pandy and Alcie.

"Okay," she said casually, "so you guys don't have any big plans for the rest of the day?"

"Zip," said Alcie.

"Zilch," Pandy agreed.

"Great. I guess, since we put into port at Iolcus tomorrow, that we'll all just relax."

"Sounds good to me," Pandy said.

"Apricots," said Alcie, flinging herself back on her sleeping cot, "I'm just gonna lie here until evening meal. Might not even get up then."

"Right," said Iole. Then she spotted a beautiful emerald bangle, which belonged to Alcie, lying on the end of the cot as if it had just been casually tossed there. "Just one more hint," she thought. "Give them just one more chance to prove they aren't complete imbeciles."

"Oh, Alce," Iole said, picking up the bracelet, "you went through so much to hide this from the pirates and guards on Atlas's mountain. By Zeus, you had to hide it in your mouth."

Pandy choked involuntarily.

"Problem?" asked Alcie, glaring.

"Nope," Pandy replied, stifling a laugh.

"It's no laughing matter, Pandy. Alcie's mouth almost wasn't big enough. Alce, you shouldn't leave this lying around. It's stunning. This is one of your Maiden Day presents, is it not?"

"Huh?" Alcie quickly grabbed the bracelet out of Iole's hands. "Oh, uh . . . no, not that one. That's just a 'Good for You, You Didn't Flunk Out of School' present."

"Well, at any rate, that must have been a special day for you. Your Maiden Day," Iole said, and then glanced at Pandy. "You, too, Pandy. Turning thirteen! I mean, not simply the presents, but the status, the importance, the recognition from your community, family . . . and friends."

"Yes, I suppose," Pandy replied, yawning. "It seems so long ago, I don't really remember."

Pandy got up off the floor and lay down on her own cot with her face toward the wall, effectively ending her part in the conversation.

"All right then," Iole said, her teeth clenched together, clomping to the far end of the room. "Well, I won't disturb you two. Have a . . . have a . . . GOOD REST!"

Throwing open the cabin door, she collided with Homer, who instantly threw his right hand behind his back and tried to look as innocent as possible as he slipped into a ridiculous, openmouthed half smile.

"Oh, hi . . . Iole. Uh, hi."

Iole just stared at him, her little chest heaving with fury.

"What?" she finally yelled.

"What, 'what'?" Homer said, confused. "I didn't say anything!"

"No, you didn't, did you!" Iole cried, marching down the corridor to the stairs leading on deck. "You most certainly *did not!*"

Homer stepped into the cabin and closed the door. Instantly Pandy and Alcie burst into peals of laughter. The ship rolled again, sending Pandy sprawling back onto the floor, and the two girls became hysterical.

"I cannot—I repeat—I cannot keep this up much longer," Alcie said. "Three times this week I came so close to spilling the broadbeans."

"It's just till tonight," Pandy said, picking herself up and sitting on her cot. "It's all prepared, right, Homer?"

"I just did, like, a final head count. All the Thracians, the Sithonian families, the two sisters from Imbros, the Roman consul to Thessaly, his wife and two of his consorts . . . uh, the third is still seasick, and the crazy cucumber salesman from Arabia and his two sons. Basically everyone Iole has even spoken to for the last six days. They can't wait. Oh, and I checked with the cook. He's making some cool veggie things for Iole and he's baking a special 'Vesuvius' cake with anise seeds around it that spell out 'You're a Maiden Now!' He's adding something called chocolate. A traveler on another ship gave him a little bit and he's been waiting for just the right time to use it. Says he's gonna heat it up and send it out of the cake like lava, and it's gonna trickle down and cover the anise seeds like they were Pompeii!"

"You're a little too excited by the lava, Homie," said Alcie.

"Fantastic! Gods, it was all so much simpler when Iole wasn't a vegetarian," Pandy said. "All right. Now, Alcie, you're giving her the bracelet . . ."

"My grammy Urania gave this to me on my Maiden Day," Alcie said as she wrapped the emerald bangle in a small piece of gauze. "But I've seen Iole looking at it when she thought I wasn't noticing; she'll love it. And Aunt Medusa accidentally turned Grammy into a statue, so it's not like she'll find out. Besides I have drawers full of stuff like this back . . . home."

Suddenly, the cabin was quiet. Everyone was thinking exactly the same thing. Alcie looked at the floor.

"We'll get *home,* Alcie," Pandy said softly, touching her friend's arm. "Your dad will buy you that girdle."

"Grape seeds, of course we will," Alcie said brightly, after a moment. She straightened her shoulders. "Homie, what'd you get her?"

"Don't laugh."

He held out his right hand.

"You got her a piece of leather?" asked Pandy.

"Unroll it," Homer said.

Alcie took the tightly rolled leather and untied the thin hemp string around it.

Together, the girls read:

GOOD FOR TEN FREE LESSONS IN THE GLADIATORIAL ARTS,
INCLUDING HACKING, PUNCHING, AND GENERAL SELF-DEFENSE.
HAPPY MAIDEN DAY!
HOMER

"I'm going to teach her to protect herself," Homer said when neither Pandy nor Alcie had spoken a word and simply stared at him.

"I love it!" Pandy said at last.

"Figs, it's brilliant," Alcie said. "But why not teach us all?"

"Because it's *her* present," Homer said, "and after what we've put her through, making her think that we all forgot, she's got to feel, like, special, y'know?"

"Oh, duh," Alcie said, then turned to Pandy. "You're up."

"I'm giving her my tortoiseshell hair clip. I don't need it. I can tuck my hair back behind my ears now anyway."

"You need your clip," Alcie said, smiling.

"I'll use a piece of leather. I'll improvise. It's Iole," Pandy said.

"That it is," Alcie said. "Very nice, my friend."

Pandy reached into her bag for the clip, but instead, her fingers found a small calfskin bag bound with a black cord.

"Huh?"

Opening it, she found a smaller calfskin bundle and a papyrus tag, which read, "To Iole, From H."

"Homie?" Alcie whirled on Homer.

"I showed you my gift. That's not from me!" Homer said.

"Let's open it," Alcie said.

"It's for Iole," Pandy replied, curiosity furrowing her brow. "But I have to know . . ."

"*H* for Hermes?" asked Alcie as Pandy opened the bundle.

"You think? But why . . . oh . . . oh!"

There in her hands lay two of the most astonishing earrings either girl had ever seen. One earring was the face of Iole's mother and the other her father, wrought in delicate curves of gold, silver, and precious stones. The hair on each seemed to actually be flowing, and the eyes, tiny agates, seemed to shift their gaze between Pandy and Alcie. Suddenly, all three realized that the faces actually *were* animated. Silently laughing, smiling, winking, and blowing kisses to each other.

"*H* is for Hephaestus!" Pandy gasped. "Only the God of the Forge could work metal into something this beautiful."

Suddenly, they heard a cry from above.

"Evening meal!"

Pandy went to rewrap the earrings and found the bundle in her hand already tied. The papyrus note attached read, "You peeked, but I forgive you. H." for a brief moment, then returned to its original message.

"Go," said Alcie, backing out of the cabin, unnerved. "Let's just go."

Pandy quickly found the hair clip and was wrapping it in a small piece of gauze on her way out of the cabin. She was thinking about the earrings and suddenly wishing that, if it meant getting presents like that, she were turning thirteen all over again.

Pandy, Alcie, and Homer searched the deck for a full ten minutes before finally coming upon Iole sitting cross-legged amidst some crates of dried goat.

"There you are," Alcie said. "Come on . . . oh . . ."

Iole didn't look at them, but they could tell right away that she'd been crying.

"Hey," Pandy said. "It's evening meal. Uh . . ."

"You all go on without me," Iole said, staring out to sea. "I'm not hungry."

"Not hungry?" Pandy said. "You only had a teeny bowl of creamed oats at first meal and nothing since then."

"I've had sufficient."

Pandy, Alcie, and Homer were at a complete loss. Iole wasn't going to budge.

"Well then," Pandy said, suddenly struck with an idea, "we'll all just sit here with you and the goat and chat, okay?"

"Yeah, I don't need to eat. Let's gab!" agreed Alcie, following Pandy's lead.

"I want to be alone . . . what goat?" Iole asked.

"You're surrounded by goat," Pandy said, pointing to the crates.

"What?" Iole said with a start.

Homer pointed to the lettering on the side of a nearby crate.

"Right here, 'Dried goat. Steam for best results.' "

"Ahhh!"

Iole bolted to her feet, her jaw set tight. At last she expelled a huge breath.

"Oh, never mind. I certainly won't be the cause of all of you not eating," she said, striding away. "It's of no consequence that nobody cares about *me*. And now I need to look before I sit anywhere!" they all heard trailing on the wind.

Approaching the dining hall on a lower deck, Alcie suddenly slipped by the others and ran swiftly ahead, disappearing though the doorway.

"Aphrodite's molars," Iole said. "What's the rush?"

"Oh," said Pandy nonchalantly, "she's just making sure that there are four seats together."

Iole didn't notice that the dining hall became silent as the three friends walked the last few meters. Pandy and Homer made certain that Iolé entered the doorway first . . .

"SURPRISE!"

CHAPTER TWO

The Boar

Iole's jaw almost hit the floor.

Every one of the nearly sixty passengers who had shared the voyage from the North African coast was in the dining hall, many with a raised goblet. Iole had charmed everyone as the ship crossed the Mediterranean, bound for Thessaly, Mt. Pelion, and other points north, with her ability to speak all their languages, her willingness to talk, and her thirst for knowledge of their countries and their stories. And just about everyone was only too willing to tell Iole of their suffering and hardship.

Kidnapped from all over the known world only weeks earlier, men, women, children—entire families— had been marched to Jbel Toubkal, the highest peak of the Atlas Mountains, and forced into hard labor. Most of the men had actually been made to lift the heavens while Pandy's uncle Atlas had succumbed to the great evil, Laziness. Bearing such a weight had caused the men to become shriveled, their skin wrinkled and burnt, although, since the evil had been recaptured, almost all were regaining their original forms.

Now most were standing tall in tribute to a young girl who had grown into maidenhood. In every other culture, Pandy realized as she stared about, this was also a special rite of passage.

"You thought we'd forgotten, didn't you?" Pandy said, putting her arms around her friend.

Iole turned to face Pandy, crying all over again.

"I'm sorry."

"Lemon rinds and olive pits," said Alcie, coming up and ushering Iole to a seat of honor in the middle of the hall, "we've planned this for days. And you hinted at it enough. Us forget? As if!"

"Hinted?" Iole said, when she'd caught her breath. "I have no idea what you're—"

"Yeah, save it," Alcie said, kissing Iole on her cheek. As the rest of the passengers dove into bowls full of tabbouleh, olives, and curried eggplant, Alcie reached into her pouch and pulled out the small gauze bundle.

"All right, before you eat . . . *presents*!"

"For *me*?" Iole said, innocently batting her eyelashes.

"Poseidon's teeth, I am so gonna smack you," Alcie said. "Mine first."

As Iole received the emerald bracelet and Pandy's

tortoiseshell hair clip, she bit her lip and tried desperately not to cry again. She knew perfectly well how precious each of these were and what they represented.

"Thank you both . . . so much," she whispered.

"Let me tie your hair back," Pandy said, reaching for Iole's long dark hair as Homer slid his scroll in front of Iole.

"Homer, you didn't have to . . . uh . . . gods . . . hacking *and* punching? I . . . oh, joy unfettered . . . I can't wait! Thank you."

Pandy reached in her bag to pull out Hephaestus's gift when she saw two little girls coming toward Iole, hands cupped, hiding their gifts. One little girl gave Iole a single red glass bead. The other girl presented Iole with the thinnest strand of pink silk, worn and frayed, which Iole recognized as having been around the girl's neck only hours before. Iole knew that anything of real value had been taken from everyone by the kidnappers in Africa, so for these two to part with such small treasures was an act of monumental generosity.

"Thank you. Here," she said softly to both, "let's put this onto this!" She strung the bead on the silk and doubled it around her wrist. "Okay?"

The two girls nodded in agreement and Iole hugged them both tightly, then looked at Pandy and Alcie, her eyes wet again.

"Sour cantaloupes," Alcie muttered to Pandy, "outdone by little plebe-os!"

"Oh please, we're all outdone by *these* . . ."

Pandy then presented the earrings from Hephaestus and Iole was stunned into silence. She stared at the faces of her parents, their lips forming the words "We love you, daughter." With great care, she put an earring on each ear, then buried her head in Pandy's shoulder and sobbed.

After a moment, Pandy felt a tapping on her arm. Turning, she found the Arabian cucumber salesman and one of his young sons.

"If I may also present a gift?" said the man, pushing his son forward. "I would like for Iole to have my son Behrooz as a husband. His name, as you may know, means 'lucky,' and that is what Iole will be if she consents to—"

"Apples," said Alcie.

Pandy's mind raced. Not only were Iole, she, and Alcie all too young to get married, the notion of Iole not making the choice herself when the time came was abhorrent.

"No, thank you," Pandy replied as Iole looked at the wide-eyed young boy, no older than she was, standing straight as one of Artemis's arrows.

"I realize she is a bit old for an arranged marriage,

but my son is easygoing. And he will inherit a nice cucumber business."

"No, it . . . it's not that," Pandy replied, pinching Iole, who had started to giggle. "It's simply . . . that . . . that . . . she's already married."

"Prunes! She is?" Alcie cried.

"I . . . I am?" Iole sputtered. "Oh, indubitably, I am . . . yes, a fine youth . . . back home. Very sorry."

"That is indeed a shame. But I honor you today, Iole."

As he and his son moved away, Iole saw the boy slump with relief, and heard him repeat, "Allah is merciful! Allah be praised!" until his father rapped him on the back of his head.

Just then, an enormous roast boar was set down in the middle of the long table directly in front of Iole and the color drained from her face.

Pandy, Alcie, and Homer panicked until the cook quickly set a platter of rice, flatbread, hummus, and vegetables at Iole's place. Taking their seats as the cook began to carve, they munched on almonds, figs, and tabbouleh until large plates of savory roast boar were passed to them. Ignoring Iole's glares, they ate quickly but normally, chewing and swallowing each bite—as did everyone—at first.

Iole was calmly spreading some green olive paste on a piece of flatbread, unaware that the entire hall had gone quiet, when she heard a strange noise. Looking up, she saw Alcie breathing hard through her nose, her mouth stuffed to bursting with meat. She no longer had the ability or room to chew. And still she was pushing meat into her mouth. Suddenly, Iole saw Pandy, her plate empty but her mouth full, reach over and take a piece of boar off Alcie's plate. Alcie slapped Pandy's hand away hard and grabbed the piece back.

Iole became still.

Instantly, Pandy was on Alcie, trying to wrestle the meat out of her hands. Iole went to stop them, but at that moment her gaze was diverted to an actual fistfight between two men that had broken out down at the far end of the table. Then, across the hall, she saw another fight between a husband and wife, and then the two Imbrosian sisters (normally so quiet) began slapping each other for the last piece of meat on a plate. Then the little girls who had given her gifts began yelling at each other and rolling on the floor, each clutching one end of a tiny rib bone.

As Iole stood, gaping at the sheer mayhem erupting throughout the hall, she saw Homer fling his empty plate to the floor, crawl up onto the table right in front of her, and begin pulling meat off the boar, filling his mouth and smearing grease and juice all over his face. In seconds, he was joined by a dozen others, screaming and shoving, all ripping meat off the carcass.

No one could get enough. The bowls of eggplant, goat cheese, and dried fruits were upended in the fracas, but no one was eating them. Everyone only wanted the meat. Iole, in shock, was roughly thrown out of the way as the cucumber salesman clambered onto the table, kicking at Behrooz to prevent him from doing the same. Homer sent one man flying across the hall in a fury. Blood was staring to flow as people gouged each other for meat. In a matter of minutes, as if attacked by a swarm of ants, the boar was laid bare. With no more meat on the bone, everyone scrambled off the table and began scouring every millimeter of the hall for scraps, leaving the white skeleton of the boar exposed.

And that's when Iole saw the small wisp of steam drifting slowly up from the rib cage, now cracked and fallen in upon itself. The boar, she knew, had been delivered hot, but not so hot as to keep anyone from eating. The juicy meat was all gone anyway, which meant there should have been no steam or smoke . . . or anything. Picking her way over people scurrying about the floor, she cautiously approached the carcass.

Climbing up onto the table, she crawled straight to the rib cage. Stifling a slight gag in her throat, she began picking through every bone. White and stripped clean, every one of them . . . yet still the steam continued to rise.

Finally, out of the very bottom of the pile, Iole spotted

a small, blackened, sizzling rib bone. She looked around at the chaos. Everyone had touched the meat, yes, but more importantly, they had all eaten it. And it affected how they ate. She'd eaten none, so touching it with her bare hands was probably all right. But she hesitated . . .

Suddenly, in her ear, she heard two tiny voices.

"Take it, daughter," said one earring.

Her mother's voice.

"All will be well," said her father.

Used to the magical ways of the gods by now, she still fought back tears of homesickness as she lunged for the bone. Grabbing it firmly, she sprang off the table and narrowly missed being walloped several times as she raced out of the hall.

She hurtled up one set of stairs, across the deck (startling a few sailors), down another set of stairs, and into her cabin. Rifling through Pandy's carrying pouch, she pulled out the wooden box and placed it on her cot next to the still-steaming bone.

She'd never done this by herself; putting the great Evils back would always be Pandy's task. This was Pandy's quest, after all; *she* had taken the box of Evils to school and *she* had accidentally let it get opened. It was somewhat understood between Pandy, Alcie, and Iole that it was Pandy's job to capture them again and physically put them in the box. But this, Iole surmised, was a lesser evil . . . overeating, perhaps, or something like that. She remembered what her parents had just said: "All will be well." Still, she hesitated. And then, out of nowhere, the full impact of the moment sent a shock through her body. This was her Maiden Day! She was no longer a girl in anyone's mind, and she could and would accept any challenge with the growing capabilities of a young woman. Besides that, there was no one else around. She indulged herself for a split second in thinking that the gods maybe, just maybe, gave this task to her and her alone. It was silly, but it didn't matter; she wasn't going to let anybody down.

She slid the hairpin from the adamant clasp, which instantly flipped up on its own. She gingerly held the black bone between her thumb and forefinger. Taking a deep breath, she opened the lid barely two centimeters, shoved the bone inside, and snapped the lid shut. Within seconds she heard the familiar sound of evil fizzling away.

She reclasped the box and slid the hairpin back into place.

Then Iole burst into tears.

"Hades' fingernails!" she scolded herself, hiccuping once. "All I'm doing is crying."

She placed the box back in Pandy's pouch, straightened her new hair clip on the back of her head, squared her shoulders, and walked out of the cabin back toward the hall, feeling like she could, from then on, do anything.

"*Happy Maiden Day to me. Happy Maiden Day to me*," she began to sing softly, a big smile on her face.

"*Happy Maiden Day, dear daughter*," her parents chimed in.

"*Happy Maiden Day to* ME!"

CHAPTER THREE

All Ashore

"Unnnhh."

"Don't try to talk," Iole said, moving toward Pandy. "Here, drink this."

"Unnn-hnnn," Pandy protested.

"Just water with a little lemon," Iole persisted.

"Where's Alcie?" Pandy asked, finding it difficult to focus.

"She's right here," Iole said, putting the water to Pandy's lips. "Pandy, it's after three on the sundial, you should eat something soon."

"I will pay you every drachma I have stashed under my pallet back home," Alcie mumbled, facedown on her cot, "if you never mention the word 'eat' again."

Alcie rolled over and raised her head against the cabin wall.

"My tongue tastes like . . . did I eat . . . a toga?"

"What happened?" Pandy asked softly. "You . . . *you* look fine, Iole."

"Where's my girdle?" Alcie cried.

"It's at the end of your cot," Iole said. "All right, last night—"

"I can't see my feet!" Alcie cried, staring at the bulge in her tummy. "Figs! I can't see my feet!"

"It's quite simple, I think. I don't eat meat anymore; it's the only reason I was spared," Iole said, then she recounted all the events of the night before from the moment the roast boar had been served to the fizzling sound of evil in the box.

"Overeating," she finished flatly. "No, more vicious than that. Binging. Gorging. One bite and you all just became ravenous."

"The lesser evil of Gorging," Alcie said.

"All by yourself? You put it in the box?" Pandy asked.

"I did."

"Nice," Alcie said.

"Very," Pandy agreed.

"When I got back to the dining hall," Iole continued, "everyone was unconscious. Homer was the first to wake, but he was still groggy. He carried you halfway to the cabin, Pandy. Then he began feeling . . . unwell . . . so he dumped you on deck and spent the rest of the night bent over the ship's railing. A lot of people were extremely, frighteningly sick. At any rate, I carried you the rest of the way."

"*You* carried me?"

"To be precise, I dragged you."

"Why does my head hurt?" asked Alcie, feeling a tender spot on the back of her scalp.

"Because I had to drag you, too," Iole said. "And even though you were basically out, you kept trying to fight me, so I dragged you by your legs. Your head kinda hit the stairs coming down. I got you both onto your cots. You just slept, Alce, but Pandy, you were incredibly sick all night, and you missed first meal, which is why I think you need to eat a little—"

"My head *bounced* off the stairs?"

"Only the back of it," Iole said, turning away, stifling a smile. "Your face is fine."

"Apricots. Iole, when I am able to get off this cot . . . ," Alcie hissed.

Just then there was a hard knock at the cabin door.

"Mid-meal," came the cook's voice, unusually gruff.

Iole hurriedly opened the door and, thanking the cook, who glowered at her as he left, took a tray with three plates and set it on the end of her cot.

"Why did he bring it to us?" Pandy asked. "Why aren't we eating in the dining hall?"

"Well, alpha, the cook doesn't want us back in the

dining hall. He feels that because I was immune to the chaos last night, I must have had something to do with it," Iole answered. "And, beta, we're the only ones left onboard, so he's basically got very little to do."

"What? Why?" Pandy asked, sitting up slowly. "Why only us?"

"Everyone, even if they still weren't feeling well, demanded to disembark on the island of Euboea early this morning, including a few of the sailors and people whose homes are even farther to the north. They all think the ship is haunted. They'd rather walk or wait for another ship. The captain would have put us off as well, but I showed him how sick you both were. Now he's just trying to sail the ship as fast as possible into the Pagasaean Gulf and to Iolcus. We must be close."

"Iole, what about the Eye of Horus? Why didn't you try that on us?" Pandy asked.

"Yeah," Alcie said. "If a tiny Egyptian amulet can heal a dead Pharaoh, or whatever, then it's good enough for me!"

"Well, first of all, it's still around Homer's neck. When I did go up to check on him periodically, he was bent so far over the railing, I couldn't get at it. And second, the eye seemed to be having no positive healing effect on him whatsoever, so I believe that the eye is basically useless on god-given injuries like the effects of a pure evil—even a lesser one; for the eye to have any effect, they have to be mortally inflicted."

"Homie!" Alcie said, swinging her legs over the side of her cot and awkwardly getting to her feet. "I've gotta find Homie!"

"Don't move too fast, Alcie!" Iole cautioned, watching Alcie hurriedly fastening her girdle.

"What do you know, head-bouncer! Oh . . . oh, Gods," Alcie cried, steadying herself before heading into the passageway.

"Come on," said Pandy, following. "We all need some air."

"Fine," said Iole. "But I'm bringing food, and you're gonna eat it."

On deck, they found Homer by the railing, passed out from sickness and exhaustion, sailors stepping over (and occasionally on) him. After Alcie had awakened him gently and gotten him standing, and after Iole had forced everyone to take a piece of dry flatbread (Alcie promptly tossed hers into the sea), they all watched the swiftly passing coastline until the ship turned to the west, rounded a hook-shaped peninsula, and headed north into a large bay.

Looking northeast, Pandy now saw two green mountains in the far distance and felt, instinctively, that one of these was their destination, Mount Pelion, and that the great plague of Lust would be hiding on it . . .

somewhere. But what form, what shape? What would she have to battle this time? Gazing at the ring of land surrounding her, she turned to the southwest and the direction of her home, knowing that at this moment, she was closer to Athens than she'd been in months. A wave of homesickness washed over her as the ship sailed farther into the bay. Closing in on the northern shore, Pandy watched the water turn from a deep blue to an emerald green, then to a light turquoise as the water became shallower.

It was only when they were one hundred meters from the gleaming white beach at the end of the bay that Pandy realized the ship had stopped moving.

She turned to say something, but Homer had his head hung over the side, still not feeling well. Alcie was adjusting her girdle for her larger-than-usual stomach, and Iole was fiddling, eyes closed, with her new hair clip. At that moment, the captain came up behind them.

"All right," he said, "all of you, off!"

"Allow us to get our belongings, sir," Pandy said.

"Be quick about it."

Ten minutes later, the four friends were back on the deck.

"Down you go," the captain said pointing to a rope ladder slung over the railing.

"Pomegranates! We're still at sea! Aren't you gonna take us to shore?" Alcie cried.

"There's silt in these waters," the captain said, looking at Alcie with a smirk. "Probably sandbars. No telling how shallow the water is, and I won't have this ship grounded for your sake," the captain said.

"What about a little boat to take us in?" Pandy asked.

"There's no silt," Homer said, looking at the clear water.

"It comes to *this*," the captain snapped. "I'm not wasting any more time on the four of you. No manpower, no boat. You can either swim the last hundred meters or you can sink. Your choice."

Homer descended first, then Alcie, then Iole and Pandy.

"Everyone okay?" Homer asked when Pandy was in the water.

"Are *you* okay?" asked Alcie.

"I'm good," Homer replied, although his tone said otherwise.

"Gods," Iole said, bobbing gently, her teeth already chattering, "I've never been a strong swimmer."

"I've got you," said Alcie.

"*I've* got her," Homer said. "Iole, like, grab hold of my belt. Alce, you good?"

"Um . . . yep."

"Pandy?"

"I'll see you on shore."

And they were off. Even though he was still unwell

and even with Iole hanging on, Homer soon outstripped Pandy and Alcie.

"I can make it, but . . . stay with me, all right?" Alcie said to Pandy between strokes.

"Not going anywhere."

Pandy remembered how Alcie had literally saved her on their last adventure, when a sudden panic attack gripped Pandy as the two girls climbed a tall column to rescue Homer. Alcie just kept talking, looking Pandy in the eye, and telling her over and over that she could "do it!" Pandy would never, in a gazillion moons, have left her friend behind in the sea, but now Pandy would carry Alcie to shore if she had to.

Lifting her face out of the water to take a breath, she saw Homer and Iole already stumbling out of the surf. Then she turned to find Alcie and realized that Alcie was many strokes behind her. She doubled back a little bit.

"You all right?" Pandy called, watching Alcie's splashy chopping motions.

"Yeah, I think so."

"What are you doing?"

"Pickled pears, what does it look like? I'm dog-paddling."

Suddenly another memory hit Pandy. She and Alcie, both age five, at Poseidon's Pee-Wee Paddlers swimming school. The other children laughing hysterically at Alcie's expensive but outlandish swim toga. Alcie using words Pandy had never heard before. The instructor making Alcie apologize. Then Alcie defiantly sitting out most of the summer months on the beach beside the sea. "Gods," Pandy thought now, "Alcie, like Iole, had never really learned to swim well!"

Pandy looked toward shore again; Iole was sitting on the sand, wringing out her soaked robes while Homer, still weak, had flopped down beside her.

Just a few more minutes and she and Alcie would be able to stand in the shallows, Pandy was certain. But looking back once more, she saw that Alcie was now starting to struggle . . . and panic. Her eyes were wild and she was beginning to take water into her lungs with every breath.

"Alcie!"

"I don't know . . . what's wrong," Alcie sputtered. "My stomach . . . I can't keep . . . swimming."

Pandy realized with a shock that Alcie was still carrying the weight from the enormous amount of meat they had all consumed the night before. And now it was exhausting her, dragging her under the surface.

"Homer!" Pandy screamed. "Homer!"

Homer looked up, startled, and instantly left Iole on the beach, racing back into the water as Alcie began flailing, straining against her heavy robes and the weight in her belly. Pandy changed course and swam after her. Alcie went under for a long moment, then her face reappeared a few meters away.

"Figs! I can't . . . !"

She tried to raise her arms, but she'd become tangled in a mass of her wet clothing like a fish in a net. Alcie went under a second time . . . and didn't come back up. Pandy changed course again, hit the spot where Alcie had been, and dove. After a few moments, she touched sand on the bottom, but Alcie was nowhere. Resurfacing, Pandy yelled at Homer, but Homer was already under. Then Homer popped up.

"Where *is* she?" Pandy screamed.

"I can't find her!" Homer yelled back.

Pandy and Homer both dove again. Pandy saw a dark object in the distant water and raced toward it, but then her eyes caught something filmy in another direction, something that might have been the color of Alcie's cloak. She headed to the surface for a quick breath, then dove again. But the shapes were gone. Then, in a completely different direction, she thought she saw something else. Utterly panicked, she turned in the sea until she didn't know which way to go. Then she spotted something behind her and swam hard, but the air in her lungs gave out before she was even close.

Breaking the surface, she spun around in the water, seeing no sign of anything. Not even air bubbles.

"There!" she heard Iole call from shore. Looking to where Iole was pointing madly, she saw Homer emerge from underneath. Then Alcie's face appeared as Homer struggled to keep her nose and mouth above water. Alcie's eyes were closed and her head bobbed lazily on her neck.

"Go in!" Homer shouted. "I've got her."

Pandy hit the beach, then both she and Iole sped back and forth in the shallow surf, frantic as they waited for Homer to bring Alcie to shore.

Finally Homer stood up in the water, carrying Alcie in his arms like she was a sack of meal. He laid her gently on the sand as Pandy and Iole crouched over her.

"Give her some room, guys!" Homer said.

But Alcie wasn't moving. Worse, she wasn't breathing, and her lips were darkening slightly.

"Whatdowedo, whatdowedo!" Pandy cried.

"Unh . . . ," Iole whimpered. "Unh . . . I think . . ."

Alcie's lips were now a medium shade of blue.

"She's dying!" Pandy screamed. And at that exact instant, she thought of something she hadn't thought of in weeks. It was all her fault. Everything. Alcie's death would sit squarely on her shoulders. They had all been working together, almost seamlessly, like a well-directed piece of theater. Reading one another's minds, knowing when and how to move, even having moments of fun on this terribly difficult quest to recapture all of the great Evils that she had stupidly loosed into the world. Pandy had pushed the enormity of her guilt to the back of her mind. Now it was the foremost thought . . . again. Fast as she could think of them, she prayed to all the gods she knew.

"Please, please, please . . . don't take Alcie!"

She slurred the words together, praying even to Hera for mercy.

"Get her girdle off!" Homer ordered.

Quickly Pandy and Iole loosened Alcie's girdle and tossed it onto the sand.

"Roll her onto her side," Homer commanded.

"Why?" Pandy shrieked.

"Just do it!"

"Homer," Iole cried, "let me have the Eye of Horus!"

Homer ripped the amulet from around his neck and tossed it to Iole. Pandy began to roll Alcie's legs as Homer rolled her shoulders. Then, standing between them, Iole bent far down to roll Alcie's waist. Her foot accidentally caught on the hem of Homer's wet robe and she stumbled forward, toppling right on top of Alcie, her hand pressing down right between Alcie's stomach and her breastbone.

"Gods!" Iole cried.

Alcie suddenly jerked up, eyes still closed, and spit out a tiny bit of water. No one moved.

"Oh," Iole whispered, clutching the eye.

Then Alcie thrashed again, threw up an *enormous* amount of water, and flopped back down on the sand. The blue color was starting to fade from her lips. Her eyes opened and she coughed and gurgled, her head rolling from side to side. She was breathing heavily. Finally, she focused on the three shadowy faces staring down at her, blocking the sun. Her brow furrowed into one long line.

"Owwww!"

"Alcie?" Pandy said, looking at her friend like she was a beached naiad.

Alcie stared hard at Pandy for a moment.

"Whaaaaaaaaaaaaat?"

"Wahooo!" said Pandy, dancing around and hugging Iole, who still hadn't moved. "You did it!"

"I thought I'd killed her," Iole said, being whirled about by Pandy like a little doll.

Homer hugged Alcie tightly, then helped her to sit. A second later, she leaned over and coughed up another huge amount of water.

"Good! Get it all out!" Homer encouraged.

"Thank you, thank you!" Pandy mouthed over and over.

Iole stepped up and gently hung the Eye of Horus around Alcie's neck.

"Anything?" Iole asked, after a few moments. "Feel better?"

Alcie looked up and nodded weakly. At last, her breathing became calmer and more regular.

"Say something, Alce . . . say anything!" Pandy begged, a huge grin on her face. "Say 'figs' or 'dates' or 'eggplant.' Tell me I'm a rotten bit of watermelon rind! Call me an apple . . . or a prune!"

"You're . . . a . . . prune."

"Yes! Yes I *am*!" yelled Pandy, jumping up and down.

"Lemon peels. I hate water," Alcie said. "And I hate boats and swimming and sand and stupid, mean captains. I hate pork . . ."

"Yay," Iole said quietly.

". . . I hate almost drowning. I hate everything."

"Good. You're fine," Pandy said, panting with relief and throwing herself down in the sand next to Alcie. "You're fine. Gods, you're fine."

All four were too shaken to really say anything for the next several minutes. Then Pandy finally raised her head.

"Now, let's see where we are."

CHAPTER FOUR

A Deal

Seeing and hearing the commotion, several people were approaching from other parts of the long, curved white beach. Two fishermen, having just unloaded their catch for the day, offered to carry Alcie farther inland, but Homer insisted that he was perfectly capable of doing that. A young mother with her two children approached Iole. After formal greetings, she explained that she had traveled from Oloosson in the north to the nearby city of Iolcus.

"There's a small tavern off this beach," she said. "We heard you all shouting from there. I'm sorry I didn't come to help sooner, but I couldn't bear to let my children see any more tragedy. There's just been so much trouble in the last few months."

"Really? Of what sort?" Iole asked, knowing perfectly well what sort. Her gaze wandered over to the boy and girl splashing in the sea, oblivious to Alcie, now being helped up by just about everyone.

"Kumquats! Stop babying me! I can stand by myself!" Alcie yelled. "Pandy . . . Pandy, will you just let go! Oh . . . oh, thank you, Homie . . . yes, if you would just take my arm . . . oh, that's it, thank you . . ."

"Looting, fistfights, greediness," the woman went on. "People I've known for years have become ill tempered and cruel. My husband is a trader doing business in the south. We're meeting him here until we decide what to do and where to go next."

"Perhaps it is just a phase of the moon, or Zeus is angry, or some such," said Iole, never considering revealing that the source of all the calamity in the world was only three meters away, sporting stringy brown hair and a soaked toga, trying to get Alcie to move slowly.

"You say there's a tavern close by?" Iole continued.

"It's just a shack, really," the woman said, pointing toward a line of trees at the edge of the beach. "For sun-worshippers, people from Iolcus with summer homes here, and the fishing trade. But I'm sure you can find something to drink there."

"Iole," Pandy said, joining them, "Alcie thinks she can walk a bit, so we're heading inland."

"Thank you," Iole said to the woman as she and Pandy moved away. "And I'm certain things won't stay this way for long. At least I hope they won't."

"Let me guess," Pandy sighed. "Somebody else affected by the box getting opened?"

"Yep. And I told her it was all your fault."

"You didn't!"

"No, I didn't."

Walking inland due north, they quickly came to a ramshackle tavern off to the side of a narrow road. Tethered close by were several donkeys, their side-bags only partially loaded with fresh fish. Off to one side, two grubby-looking men were watering two tired-looking cows, each attached to a low cart. The men were arguing halfheartedly about nothing in particular. Then Pandy saw a large oxcart across the road; a tarp covered what looked like rotting hay in the back.

"The Odyssey," Iole said, reading the sign posted over the tavern entryway. "Well, it's fitting."

"I know," Pandy agreed. "Like Odysseus, most of the time I don't know what's around the next corner for us."

Inside, several fishermen gave the girls a more-than-casual glance, then saw Homer standing behind them and quickly looked away. As fishermen bartered and bargained with fishmongers, Alcie read a sign over the counter.

"Iolcus is that-a-way," Alcie said, pointing to the

city's name and a crude arrow burnt into the board. "Doesn't say how far. Wish there was a sign for Mount Pelion."

"What do you want?" asked a scruffy barman with a giant, jutting belly.

"Gods!" Iole said out of the side of her mouth. "I just realized we have no money."

"What was that?" said the barman.

"Hang on," Pandy said, digging through her carrying pouch. Finally, she withdrew a single copper coin and triumphantly laid it on the counter.

"Four glasses of juice, my good man!"

"That will get *you* a single glass of water with a little lemon twist," the barman sneered. "Now, if you're not going to order more than that, get out."

"Look," Pandy said quickly. "We really just need some information."

"What kind of information?" said the barman, subtly placing his calloused hand over the coin.

"We just need to know how to get to Mount Pelion," Pandy replied.

"Is that all?" said the barman. "Well, I think information should be free of charge, don't you?"

"Yes, I do," said Pandy, reaching for the copper coin.

"But," the man said, tossing the coin into the air and catching it in a fold of his robe, "it's not. Talk to the puny guy over there in the corner. He's from a village on

Pelion, I guess. Came in here just before you did, cryin' like a baby about how he was waylaid by thieves on his journey down the mountain and now has no money to pay for fish. Maybe you can hop a ride with him. I think he'll probably have room."

"Oh, yes," Iole muttered as the barman laughed and walked away. "People are pleasant."

"Come on," said Pandy.

In the far corner, they found a very short, extremely thin man staring, red-eyed, out of an open window.

"Excuse me, sir," Pandy began. "I don't mean to bother you . . ."

"Bother me?!" the man shrieked. "That's very funny. As if I could be bothered further. My village saves for weeks to buy supplies, and now I have to go back up that infernal mountain, and tell them we're all going to starve! How could you bother me further?"

"By asking for a ride," Alcie said, without missing a beat.

"What?" the man fairly screamed.

"Sir." Pandy paused to speak calmly. "We just thought that if you were going up the mountain anyway, we might accompany you. We could certainly protect you on the way back, and we could tell your entire village of the trouble you encountered. Homer here would . . . uh, beat up . . . anyone who tried to beat you up."

"Can you pay me?" the man asked quickly.

Pandy looked at the others.

"All our good stuff was taken on Atlas's mountain, remember?" said Alcie.

"And I just used my last coin," Pandy said. She turned back to the man.

"No, sir, we can't pay you," she said simply. "I guess we'll walk. Thanks anyway."

"It's over a week walking. If you don't get eaten. Or worse," he said, a slight gleam in his eye now. "Are you sure you have nothing?"

"Uh, no," Pandy said.

"I disagree," he said, smiling.

Then she slowly followed his gaze to Iole's wrist.

"That will get you all up the mountain and then some!" he hissed, making tiny pointing motions toward Iole's new emerald bracelet.

Iole instinctively hid her hand behind her back.

"Don't even think about it!" Alcie said to the man.

"It was a present," Iole whispered.

"Have a nice walk," the man said, turning back to the window.

Iole looked at Pandy. Pandy smiled at her.

"You don't have to, Iole. We'll get there."

"That's right!" Alcie said. "Moldy apples, that's right. My grammy Urania gave me that and I gave it to you. No way does he—"

"Alcie," Iole said softly, "be quiet."

Iole closed her eyes for a moment, then brought her arm forward and slowly removed the bracelet.

"As if!" Alcie yelled.

"Alcie . . . shhhhh!" Pandy said.

"I gave that to you!" Alcie mouthed.

"And now I have to give it up, Alce," Iole said. Turning her head to the side, she whispered, "Nothing—no bracelet, no present—nothing is worth delaying what we're doing."

"Figs!"

"Thank you, Iole," Pandy said. "Thank you."

"It was great for a day," Iole said.

"I am never speaking to you again," Alcie said, turning and clomping out of the tavern.

"Alcie!" Iole called, running after her.

Twirling the bracelet on one finger, the man grinned at Pandy and Homer before dropping it into a leather pouch.

"Eteocles, that's my name. And now, if you'd like to get started, my oxcart awaits."

"Don't you want to use the bracelet to buy some fish?" Pandy asked dryly. "You could buy tons."

"All the decent fish are gone now," Eteocles sniffed. "Besides, this will buy a whole new life for me."

"What about your starving village?" Homer asked.

"What about them? Let them starve. I'll take you to the mountain and then it's off to Persia or Rome for me!"

"What if we tell your village what you did?" Pandy said.

"What if I drop you an hour's walk from my village? That's a nice head start, I think. Now, do you want to continue this conversation here or on the road?"

Pandy turned and walked toward the door, but Homer blocked Eteocles' way.

"That bracelet is worth way more than a ride up a mountain," Homer said.

"Your friends don't seem to think so," Eteocles replied, trying to get around Homer.

"It would be only, like, a couple of coins to hire a chariot in any city," Homer said, sidestepping quickly.

"Then I suggest you find a city and hire a chariot," Eteocles said. "Iolcus is fairly close. Why don't you and your friends—"

Homer bore down on the man.

"I don't like seeing people I care about getting cheated. What's to keep me from taking that bracelet right now, flattening you, and taking your team and cart? Huh?" Homer asked, his eyes cold and his voice low.

Eteocles stopped in his tracks and stared up at Homer.

"First," he said softly, "the deal was made between myself and the girl. Second, you must certainly be aware that appearances can be deceiving. I might have reserves of strength and agility that are belied by my small, wasted exterior."

Something in the man's eyes made Homer take a step back.

"And third," the man said, brightening slightly, "your code of honor, my friend. You would never do such a thing."

Following Eteocles out of the tavern, Homer saw Pandy and Iole petting the two old oxen yoked to the cart, and Alcie, in the opposite direction, staring straight up toward the sky.

"Alcie, come on!" Pandy called.

With a giant heave of her shoulders, Alcie turned and walked to the cart, looking straight down. Arranging themselves on the dirty tarp, Alcie made certain that she was staring anywhere but at Iole.

"We have quite a ride ahead . . . get comfortable!" Eteocles called over his shoulder. And they were off.

The forest became denser and greener the higher they climbed. Occasionally, Pandy spotted a cave or a small waterfall, but there were very few signs of life on the mountain. With four extra bodies to haul, the oxen were quickly spent and Homer had to jump off several times and help push the cart over bumps and out of deep ruts.

He quickly realized he needed to walk alongside if they were going to make any progress.

Late that afternoon, Homer and Eteocles went off in different directions to hunt for game, while Alcie and Iole gathered twigs and Pandy started a fire. Homer came back empty-handed, but Eteocles had caught two rabbits and three wild birds, which made a tasty evening meal for everyone except Iole.

Alcie, still not speaking to Iole, made certain that she sat close to her and, as Iole ate some dried dates and figs, casually and "accidentally" waved bits of rabbit in front of Iole's nose.

As the moon rose, the girls curled up on top of the tarp, their cloaks spread like blankets. Eteocles slept on the ground while Homer kept watch.

At dawn the next morning, after a quick first meal, they were back on the road. The incline grew very steep very fast, and one by one, the girls all joined Homer at the back of the cart, pushing and pulling with the oxen.

"This is ridiculous!" Alcie whispered as they lay on the tarp that night. "What in Hades did we pay for? We could have walked up here faster."

"We're eating well," Pandy said, still marveling at the animals that Eteocles had snared for that evening's meal. Homer had again come back empty-handed, but Eteocles had caught a small goat and several wild hares.

"And I don't know what he's using to catch anything," Alcie said.

"Must be his hands," Iole said. "Disgusting."

"Everyone up!" Eteocles was shouting the next morning. Pandy woke with a start. She'd been dreaming that Athena was offering her some ambrosia and nectar, saying, "Come on! Become immortal . . . you know you want to!" Suddenly waking up, surrounded by tall trees, she had no idea where she was. Alcie's palm accidentally mashed down on Pandy's wrist as Alcie lifted herself off the tarp.

"Ow!" Pandy said, and instantly she remembered that she was somewhere on Mount Pelion, looking for Lust.

"Sorry," Alcie said, jumping down off the cart.

Once more, after a hasty first meal of creamed oats ("Where did he get oats?" Pandy had whispered to Iole. "I always keep a spare pouch handy," Eteocles had called out), they were off again. Alcie stubbed her toe, then Iole twisted her ankle, then Pandy tripped getting the cart out of a hole and landed on her face; she was getting more and more frustrated. But they had only walked for a few hours when Eteocles brought the oxen to a halt.

"Very well," Eteocles began.

"Is this where you drop us off and get that hour's head start?" Pandy asked snidely.

Even Alcie looked at her.

"Touchy this morning, aren't we?" Eteocles replied.

"We've walked for, basically, two days," Pandy said, her anger rising. "We could have done that ourselves."

"You wouldn't have known where to go if you'd been by yourselves," Eteocles answered, his voice calm.

"We'd have gotten here," Alcie said.

"We actually helped you get this cart up the mountain. We don't mind paying, but not for something unfair. You need to give back the bracelet," Pandy said firmly.

Eteocles paused for a second, then threw back his head and laughed. Pandy saw a strange, thin pale line zigzag down his face. Then another. All at once, he began to grow. As he became larger and larger, his wrinkled brown skin began to crack, peel away, and drop to the ground, revealing taut, perfect white skin covering bulging muscles. The dirty toga was transformed into a clean, bright, silvery fabric, and the grayish hair became golden and curly, topped with a beautiful winged helmet.

"Down!" Pandy cried to the other three, who were staring, stupefied.

Instantly, all four were on their knees, heads bowed.

"Pears! Is that who I think it is?" Alcie whispered.

"Yes! Shhhh!" Pandy hissed back.

After a second of silence, she lifted her eyes.

"Okay, missy," Hermes said with a grin, his arms

folded across his massive chest, staring straight at her. "You are getting *spunky*!"

"I'm so sorry," Pandy began.

"What's with the 'sorry'?" Hermes said. "I like it! All right . . . everybody up!"

Instantly, Pandy and the rest were on their feet.

"Eyes on me."

Everyone looked straight at Hermes.

"Try not to look terrified," Hermes said to the group as he walked toward Alcie.

"Hello, Alcestis," he said softly, and then turned to the others. "Oh, I just realized . . . Pandora is the only one who's actually met me. And yet I feel like I know all of you so well."

"Mighty Hermes, swift and fleet footed," Alcie began.

"Yes, Alcestis, thank you. I know," Hermes said. "You're doing very nice work."

"Uh, thanks," Alcie said.

"Homer," Hermes said, approaching the youth. "Now, aren't you glad you didn't try to flatten me? It would have gotten out of hand . . . probably a little ugly. But you kept your cool and, hey, good times!"

"Uh . . ."

"I like you, Homer. We all do. Not the brightest lamp in the temple, but you have heart. And a noble soul."

"Yes. Thank you. I think," Homer said.

"Well, you try to and that's what matters. Hello, Iole."

"Wondrous Hermes . . ."

"Ach, can't anyone just say 'hello'?" Hermes rolled his eyes. "Okay, enough! Now, instructions first, questions afterward. I could be all godlike and get a little flowery but that would get us nowhere fast, and since you all need to get somewhere fast, I'll put it to you straight. You're going back in time. All of you. Many centuries. What you seek has traveled the river of ages—sorry, that was flowery. I'm going to get you there and bring you back, that's if you're all still alive. Here's the rule: don't change anything in the past or it will alter the future. Seriously. And it might not be good. Any questions?"

"Uh, yes," Iole said, thinking fast, as the others just looked at one another, confused. "How far back are we going?"

"Roughly thirteen centuries. Next?"

"Lust is . . . is . . . back in time?" Pandy asked.

"Alcie, what's the word you always say when somebody says something obvious? Starts with a delta, I think," Hermes asked.

"Uh, 'duh'?"

"That's it! Duh!"

"Are you going to stay with us?" Pandy asked.

"Let me put it this way. I'll be there, and I'll know you're you, but don't look to me for help of any kind until and only if you're ready to come back."

"Oh!" gasped Iole suddenly.

Hermes stared at her for a second.

"You have it, don't you?" he asked.

"Mount Pelion . . . thirteen hundred years ago," she started.

"Give or take," Hermes said casually.

"Oh! Oh! And they're *all* going to be here?"

"What? Who!" Alcie cried, whacking Iole on her arm.

"Almost all," said Hermes, smiling. "Someone's missing. But then, you knew that, didn't you?"

"Iole?" Pandy said, looking at her quizzically.

"Enough gab," Hermes said. "Time's a'wasting, and how. Everybody grab a little piece of my toga—don't get fresh—and we'll be off."

Pandy, Alcie, Iole, and Homer each pinched a small amount of the silver fabric and instinctively braced themselves for a whirlwind journey back through time. Alcie and Iole hunched over as if preparing to face a horrible hurricane. Pandy clutched her pouch to her chest and planted her feet firmly on the ground. Homer grabbed his cloak with his free hand and closed his eyes, head down.

"Alcie, Iole . . . what are you doing?" Hermes asked.

"We're hanging on. Won't there be wind . . . or something?" Alcie yelled.

Pandy, looking at her toes, saw a small shift, a subtle repositioning of the stones on the ground around her feet. She noticed that the birds that had been singing were silenced, and a small white boulder had materialized on a patch of grass off to her left . . . and then nothing.

"You four are crazy!" Hermes laughed. "You look like you're about to be attacked! It's done. We're there."

"That's it?" Pandy asked, looking around.

"That's it," Hermes said.

"I just thought there would be . . . wind," Alcie said, standing up straight.

"You're . . . ," Pandy began.

"I'm what? Fabulous?" Hermes asked.

"No. I mean, yes! But you're *helping*." Pandy's voice dropped to a whisper on the last word.

"I did, and I might again," Hermes said. "Now don't blow it by asking a lot of questions."

The forest surrounding them was essentially the same. Some trees were taller, some were smaller, and some were new. There was a different cloud formation in the sky, but there was no other marked visible difference.

"I'm off," Hermes said, then pointed east. "Your way lies down that road. Remember, change nothing."

He stepped back and Pandy thought he was about to disappear when he stopped and turned to Iole.

"You're kidding, right?"

Iole's mouth fell open and then she looked down at the ground.

"I'm sorry."

"At a time like this, *that's* what you're thinking about?" Hermes asked. I would have expected that of Alcie, not you."

"Huh?" Alcie said.

"I'm sorry," Iole said again.

"A deal is a deal, Iole. It doesn't matter that I probably can't use it. So, no, you can't have the bracelet back."

Iole nodded.

Hermes shook his head and disappeared in a bright white flash.

"Nice going, Miss I-Can-Give-Away-My-Presents," Alcie said after a pause. "Now he hates us!"

"No he doesn't, Alcie. Quit it," Pandy said. "Iole, what in Zeus's name is going on? What do you know?"

"Did either of you *ever* pay attention when Master Epeus was teaching ancient Greek history? *Ever?* Thirteen hundred years ago, Zeus was in love with the goddess Thetis. Hera found out about it and got so angry that not only did she force Zeus to stop seeing Thetis, she made Zeus give Thetis to a mortal man as his wife."

"Oh, yeah! I was awake for this," Pandy cried. "King Peleus! Whose palace is . . . was . . . is on Mount Pelion!"

"Correct!" Iole continued. "It was a huge celebration to which all the gods and goddesses were invited."

"Except one," Pandy said.

"Correct again. And if my guess is right, today is the big—"

"Do you think you have been hired to simply stand around!"

A shrill voice, like the sound of a horn, high and off-key, pierced the quiet of the forest. Pandy, Alcie, Iole, and Homer whipped their heads around.

Then their jaws dropped.

CHAPTER FIVE

On Staff

"As if I don't have enough to worry about!"

The shortest, roundest woman Pandy had ever seen was ambling toward them. Pandy assumed she was moving by herself, although she couldn't see the woman's feet. Her girth was easily that of a large chariot, and the top of her head, Pandy calculated, came only to the top of Pandy's shoulder. Her silvery hair, however—swept up, fastened and held in place with myriad combs and pins—towered easily another meter above that. Her lips and eyelids were painted a pale green, and she was wearing a long leaf-colored gown, covered by a dark green robe. She was breathing hard and sweating profusely.

"Gods," Alcie said. "It's a walking squash."

"The Messenger God himself had to come and tell me that I had four slackers out on the road, taking their own precious time! The other servants I ordered managed to arrive early and got straight to work. But lucky me, I had to get a few troublemakers, didn't I? Today of all days! Certainly you have been told of the importance of this occasion? That everything must go off perfectly, with precision and flair? Consummate celebrations! That is what Events by Echidna is known for, and I will not have four temporary servants ruin my reputation. I warn all of you now," she said, glaring at them, "Midas's Golden Touch Temp Agency will hear from me if any of you so much as looks in the wrong direction, and I will personally see to it that you are shipped off to Troy to rebuild the citadel brick by brick. Do I make myself clear?"

"Yes," Pandy said immediately.

"To *everyone*?" she barked.

"Yes!" said Alcie, Iole, and Homer.

"Good!"

The woman, Echidna, slowly waddled around the group, gazing up and down.

"Where are your serving togas?"

"Um . . . we only have what we're wearing," Pandy said, thinking fast.

"What?" she gasped.

"We had to walk the last several kilometers. It's been very dusty," Iole chimed in.

"Where are your armbands? Your serving armbands? The ones that say 'Need something? Just ask!' Where are they?"

"We lost them," Alcie said.

Echidna began to turn red.

"This is the last time I use Midas, I can promise you," she sputtered. "Very well, follow me. Fortunately I always come prepared for any situation. Hurry!"

Pandy and the rest leapt forward to follow, but Echidna moved so slowly that they could all remain several steps behind and walk at an easy pace.

"What are we doing?" Alcie asked Pandy quietly.

"First of all," Pandy whispered back, "she said that Hermes told her we were here. I'm guessing that means we're supposed to go with her. Second, what better way to get into this event? See what's going on for ourselves. We don't have invitations. Hermes wouldn't have brought us back in time to this location unless Lust was somewhere close by. He said so himself. This is perfect!"

"So we simply have to ascertain someone or something that is consumed with a burning, insatiable, voracious, and unquenchable desire for someone or something else," Iole said softly. "Correct?"

"Did all those words mean the same thing?" Alcie asked.

"Somebody wants something really badly," Iole replied, rolling her eyes.

"Can I pinch her, Pandy?" Alcie asked, seeing the look. "Can I pinch that big brain right out of her head!"

"Stop it, Alce, and yes, that's what we're looking for," Pandy whispered. "I'm certain that's why we're at this particular event."

"What, exactly, is this event that you two know about?" Alcie asked. Unfortunately, she asked it just a little too loudly, and Echidna whirled around.

"What is this event!"

"Oooops," mumbled Alcie.

"It is one of the final, yet most important, stages of the wedding of King Peleus to Silver-Footed Thetis, which is only the premiere social event of the season, you silly girl!" Echidna was on the march again, speaking to the others (and herself) as if she were rattling off a checklist. "The bride has made her procession from her family home to the home of her husband, then came the wedding feast this afternoon—a little backward, I know, but I like to shake things up a bit when catering to the needs of my clients. Now all we have left is the formal unveiling! And, since it's going to be in the main hall, I needed more staff, which is where you slackers come in. Pass a few trays, off comes the bridal veil, collect my fee, then I'm giving my feet a nice long soak. All right . . ."

Echidna stopped at a fork in the path. Two tall, impossibly thin women approached from the path to the right.

"Hypatia, take this youth and give him a fresh toga

and rustle up an armband. He's rather thick; you might have to sew two together. He'll work the wine bar. Ireneus, get this dark-haired one cleaned up and give her to Thetis. Apollo's big toe, that goddess needs all the help she can get. And Ireneus, when you're done, bring two fresh serving togas down to the cave. You . . ."

Echidna turned to Iole.

"You will help the bride with whatever she needs. You will help her attendants, you will not speak to anyone, and you will stay out of the way. Understood?"

"Absolutely," said Iole.

"Both of you, this way," Hypatia said as she and Ireneus led Homer and Iole off.

"You two come with me," Echidna said, motioning for Pandy and Alcie to follow. After several minutes of walking very slowly, Alcie couldn't help herself—she started silently mimicking Echidna's walk, then she would lie down on the path and pretend to sleep, then wake with a start and rush to catch up, or lean against a tree, fall asleep, then rush to catch up, or pretend to run in place. Pandy started laughing so hard she had to hit Alcie to make her quit. It was only fifty or so meters from the fork in the path, but it was easily ten minutes before Echidna finally rounded a large tree trunk and stopped.

"Whoa!" said Pandy.

"Oranges!"

Across a small clearing was the entrance to an enormous black cave.

Many servants were rushing to and fro, like oversized ants, carrying trays, bowls, large stirring spoons, huge ladles, and so forth. Everyone's hair was tied tightly back away from his or her face, which was flushed and glowing with nervous tension and heat from several enormous cooking cauldrons. From inside the cave could be heard much shouting, orders being called out and answered. Suddenly, there was a scream, followed by the loud clang of something falling over, and a big puff of smoke filled the opening.

A wild-looking black-haired youth shot out of the cave and headed toward Echidna, furiously waving his hands. He was wearing an officious-looking white silk headband.

"I cannot work with him in there, Echidna!" he screeched. "I cannot bring out the very essence of my culinary creations if he's going to be pawing through everything! We're in a cave . . . a *cave*! And he's literally trampling on my genius!"

"Myron . . . Myron, calm down," Echidna said, using a low, even voice for the first time. "It is his home, after all."

At that moment, scattering servants in all directions, a colossal centaur raced through the cave opening, a giant skewer of meat in one hand. Turning quickly on his hind legs, he threw the roast on its red-hot metal spit back into the crowd of workers, sending them flying.

"Oh!" Pandy nudged Alcie. "This . . . this is fantastic! Alcie, do you know who that is?"

"You deal with him, Echidna," Myron said, tears forming in his eyes as he walked off into the woods. "I am simply too spent. And my heart is just broken."

Echidna sighed heavily.

"Excuse me," she said, cautiously crossing to the centaur, now pacing back and forth before the cave opening. "Excuse me, Master Chiron?"

"Figs," said Alcie quietly.

"You know it," Pandy agreed. Even Pandy had stayed awake when Master Epeus had talked about Chiron, without question the most famous and important centaur in Greek history. Whereas other of these half man–half horse beings were infamous for their savagery, Chiron was known for his wisdom and kindness. He was so learned that many noble and wealthy families sent their sons to be raised by this marvelous creature, his most famous pupil being Hercules.

"They're making a mess!" The centaur galloped to her, the veins in his lower body pulsing through his black horsehair. "I have tried to be patient. But they're using my private food stores, my private utensils. They've even disrupted my library! I was told my private things would be left alone!"

"I know, and you're right. I will put a stop to that nonsense immediately. But we both know how important this day is. And there is truly no space in the palace," Echidna said, beginning to purr. "So if you would just be a little indulgent, I promise you we will leave everything just as we found it. You will never know we were even here!"

Chiron ran his hands through his bushy black hair and pawed at the ground.

"The things I do for my king," he snorted. "And I wasn't even invited!"

"I'll work on that," Echidna answered quickly. "I'll see what I can do . . . maybe a nice spot on an upper balcony somewhere?"

Chiron looked at her like she was a little bug. Then he slowly moved off to a large, flat rock and settled down, staring out at the forest.

"Myron!" Echidna called. "Myron, it's fine now. Come back."

"You cannot tell me, Echidna," he said, flouncing back, hands on his hips, "that in that lovely, massive palace there isn't just one corner for me? I have never been forced to work culinary miracles in a cave!"

"Myron, we have already been over this," Echidna said calmly. "The rooms are all being used, every one of them. The bride's family alone is using every last sleeping pallet, and they're sleeping five to a room, Myron.

Naturally, the gifts had to go somewhere out of sight, and the only space left was the food preparation room. It will all be over tomorrow. Be a love and say you understand?"

Myron closed his eyes and rubbed his forehead.

"I cannot *tolerate* much more of this, Echidna," he choked out dramatically. His eyes were moist as he slowly backed away, beating lightly on his chest, as if his burden was almost too much to bear. "I am an artist . . . an *artist*!"

"Yes, Myron. But dear, it's day two. No more big feasts, just nibblies to keep the immortals happy during the unveiling of the bride! You don't have to put so much stress on yourself."

"Stress is my life!" Myron said, throwing his arms in the air as he walked back into the cave.

"Aphrodite's toenails . . . let me make it through this. All right, you two." Echidna turned to Pandy and Alcie. "Start putting canapés on serving trays. When Ireneus brings your fresh togas and armbands, put them on. You can stow your clothing and accoutrements here at the staging area. The guests will start arriving in twenty minutes by my calculation of the sundial, and I want the two of you at the palace, trays in hand and ready. Understood?"

"Yes," Pandy said.

"Got it," said Alcie.

Echidna moved off, and Pandy heard her muttering something about a vacation in Syria.

Pandy was walking toward the cave opening when she realized that Alcie wasn't beside her. Looking back, she saw Alcie walking slowly toward Chiron, now dozing peacefully.

"Master Chiron?" Alcie said softly.

"Hmmph?" the centaur woke with a start.

"I have to tell you that you are, without question, one of my favorite historical figures. I actually paid attention in class when Master Epeus talked about you. I just wanna ask . . . how cool was it to work with some of those heroes of the Trojan War? I mean, one of the greatest was—"

"The what?" Chiron asked.

"The Troj—"

Pandy grabbed Alcie by her arm and jerked her away.

"I'm sorry, sir," Pandy said. "She gets a little insane when she hasn't eaten. Sorry to bother you."

"What?" said Alcie as Pandy pushed her toward the cave.

"The Troj—the TW obviously hasn't *happened* yet, you doofball!"

"Uh-oh."

"Yeah! Nice going. You probably just changed history, and now we won't be born!"

CHAPTER SIX
Odd Jobs

After finding Homer a clean white serving toga (size extra-large, and it was still a little tight), Hypatia led him over to the main wine bar in the great hall of King Peleus's palace.

"You'll work here, behind this bar," Hypatia said, her eyes bulging out of her razor-thin face. Her voice was crisp and she pronounced her words slowly and perfectly. "You will speak to no one except to say that we are serving four delightful wines. A hearty red with a hint of oak and berries. A lighter red, slightly brassy, with a touch of lavender. An amusing pink with lashings of citrus and cedar. And finally a white with hints of fern and a sassy, naughty attitude! The wineskins are not labeled because that would be tacky, so get familiar with each one before the guests arrive. Get them confused, and I will have you flogged. I'll send someone to help you."

Homer, having said nothing, watched her walk away, then he bent underneath the bar to inspect the wineskins.

Several minutes later, he heard a voice above him calling hello. Raising his head, he collided with the bar and lifted it off its base.

"Oh, hey! Sorry, I didn't mean to frighten you! Here, let me help."

A slender, brown-haired youth of about Homer's age rushed to grab one end of the marble bar and set it back in place.

"Thanks," said Homer, rubbing his head.

"I'm Dimitris of Cyphus."

"Homer of Crisa."

"Crisa? Huh. Never heard of it."

Homer suddenly realized that there was a very strong chance that Crisa hadn't yet been established as a thriving seaport.

"It's small."

"Well, it's nice to know you," Dimitris said. "The skinny woman who looks like a chicken said you'd tell me everything I need to know."

"Oh, okay. Well, there are, like, four wines. One tastes like a flower, two taste like trees, and the last one has a bad attitude. And you can't talk to anybody."

Iole, who had been standing in a corner of the bridal dressing room for twenty minutes, was somewhat surprised (and a little pleased) to learn that, even after all her adventures and everything she had witnessed in the last few months, she still had the capacity to be . . . shocked. After she had dressed in a fresh toga and run a damp cloth over her grimy arms and legs, Ireneus had all but shoved her into the bridal dressing suite. It was a beehive of activity; half a dozen maidens, clothed just like Iole, were rushing around the edges of the rooms with goblets and ewers of water and wine, plates of delicacies, and armloads of clothing. She was almost knocked over as two maidens raced up to Demeter (whom Iole recognized by Pandy's description of her ever-changing hair), who was reclining next to Calliope, the muse of epic poetry, and Euterpe, the muse of lyric poetry, on a divan close to the bride's dressing table. The maidens presented Demeter with two different golden outer robes for the bride to wear. Demeter chose one and the girls ran off again.

Initially Iole had tried to help. She called to the passing girls as they rushed by but was told to just stay out of the way, so now she stood, almost motionless, mesmerized by the real activity in the center of the room.

Four of the most beautiful, pale-skinned nymphs Iole had ever seen stood in a wide semicircle around the seated bride, Silver-Footed Thetis. In the center of this semicircle was a giant slow-spinning vortex: brushes, pins, combs, red-hot hair irons, tiny clips, pots of hair wax, and all manner of decorative hair jewels and accessories were whirling through the air. With a mere flick of their fingers, the nymphs would send a brush or a comb to do their bidding. At a gesture from one nymph, Thetis's long, silver hair swept itself up into an intricate pile of curls and dangling ringlets. Not liking the style, the nymph let it fall. Then they braided the hair and coiled it like a serpent on top of Thetis's head. Again, the nymphs shook their heads and the hair cascaded down Thetis's shoulders. Up, down, poofy, flat . . . style after style they tried, as Demeter and the muses called out suggestions. Iole watched all of this, entranced. But what truly amazed her was the bride herself.

Thetis sat at her dressing table before an enormous mirror, sobbing like a child who had just been spanked.

She was surrounded by everything any goddess could desire on her wedding day: dozens of pots, jars, bottles, and bowls. There were smoothing creams, colored powders for her eyes, crushed berries for her cheeks and lips, black kohl for her lids, and several glorious perfumes. There were resplendent golden garments (the traditional color, Iole knew, of every bride on her wedding day), willing handmaidens, and a celebration on the horizon. And yet, by Iole's reckoning, the bride was a complete and utter mess.

"I . . . just . . . just . . . don't understand why I had to get . . . *m-m-married*!" she wailed. No one in the room was actually paying any attention to Thetis's cries, concentrating more on simply getting her ready to walk through the hall.

"Huh?" she choked. "C-c-could someone just exp-p-plain that to me?"

"Because Hera wanted it and Zeus decreed it, darling," Demeter said, not looking away from the maiden at her feet and the two girdles she was deciding between. "Amethysts . . . hmmm? They *are* royal, but for the final unveiling, I'm just not seeing it. Let's go with the diamonds, shall we? Gold with diamonds. Elegant and tasteful."

"Thetis," Euterpe said, "didn't we all have fun last night at your proaulia? Huh? The feast your father held was a wonderful kickoff! The food was great, all your sisters were there, and you made some wonderful sacrifices to Artemis, Aphrodite, and Hera."

Iole knew they were talking about the first evening of what would be a three-day event and wondered what Thetis had offered up to the goddesses to ease her transition into marriage and child-rearing.

"And Peleus's sacrificing a bull to Zeus was a nice touch," Calliope said.

"Oh, G-G-Gods! Zeus!" Thetis wailed. "I thought he l-l-loved me!"

69

"Yes, sweetheart, but there is a tiny problem in that he's *already married*," Demeter said, rolling her eyes.

"You and Peleus were so lovely together at today's feast. And I think that puffy wedding planner was smart to insist on having a little rest. I'm enjoying the changes she's made to the traditional ceremony. But now you've made the procession to this nice, big palace, the guests are gathering again, and all you have left is for your father to hand you over to Peleus and then the formal unveiling," Calliope said.

"You're practically home free!" Euterpe sang out. "And don't forget tomorrow—your epaulia! Lots and lots of presents!"

"I say the sandals with bronze and copper tones," Demeter said, looking at several pairs. "They'll show off her silver feet. Girls? What do you say?"

Euterpe and Calliope agreed. Thetis let out a particularly loud cry, and Euterpe, who was known for being almost deliriously chipper no matter what the occasion, decided to try change the subject.

"Peleus is marvelously handsome, Thetis," she said cheerfully. "Don't tell the Supreme Ruler that I said this, but I think he's handsomer than Zeus! Just think of the adorable children you'll have!"

"Ahhhhhhhhhhhh!"

It was at this moment that Iole decided Lust was

nowhere in this room. No one (especially the bride) was displaying a burning desire for anything.

"Oh hush, Thetis," Calliope said. "Rubies and pearls at the neck, thank you, maiden. Thetis, it's already been foretold. You're giving birth to heroes . . . at least one, so buck up!"

At this, Thetis seemed to calm down a touch. She popped numerous sticks of clove-and-nutmeg chewing sap into her mouth and sat chomping away for a minute.

"Heroes, huh?"

"That's what we've heard, my dear," said Calliope.

"Well, it's a nice consolation prize, I guess. And you know what? I had already picked out a couple of cute baby names for when Zeus and I . . . I . . . oh . . ."

She began to sniffle.

"Don't start in crying again, honey!" Euterpe called. "You'll run the rest of that kohl right down your face. Let's hear those names!"

"Well, I've always liked Carpus or Cleon for boys."

Completely involuntarily, Iole gasped hard, and before she knew what she was doing, opened her mouth.

"NO!"

Every eye in the room turned to look at the little dark-haired maiden standing in the corner.

Although she was thinking faster than she ever had, even Iole simply could not come up with a way to cover her blunder. There was no hope of saying something like, "Oh! I just meant, 'Oh, that's great!'" Her objection had been too loud and too distinct.

"You have a better idea, servant?" asked Thetis.

Iole knew, and she was the only in the room who did, that Thetis was destined to mother perhaps the greatest of Greek heroes, next to Hercules.

"Yes," she said clearly, realizing that it was a celebration day, after all, and they probably wouldn't kill her . . . maybe just torture her a bit. "Yes, I do. Um. A beautiful goddess and a great king who will have a strong and powerful heir should have a strong and powerful name. I . . . uh . . . on my way here, I stopped at the Oracle at Delphi."

Several ohs went through the room.

"That's *right*! Very important. And the high priestess agreed to see me. I told her I was coming here. And she offered, through me, to you . . . as a gift on your wedding day . . . the name of your most famous child."

"Yes?" Thetis asked.

"Achilles."

The name rippled through the crowd and everyone nodded her head. Even Demeter, Calliope, and Euterpe seemed pleased.

"Why didn't she tell one of my guests—one of the important ones? Why did the high priestess tell *you*?" Thetis asked, arching one eyebrow.

"I . . . have absolutely no idea," Iole said.

Thetis paused, gazing darkly at Iole. Then she shrugged her shoulders.

"Well, it doesn't matter. It *is* better than Cleon, I suppose."

Everyone softly agreed.

"Okay, I like it. And just for that, you can carry the ends of Demeter's hair as she walks before me . . . whoever you are."

"What's with the look?" Alcie asked Pandy as they trudged up a small hill.

"Huh?" Pandy replied.

"The look? You look more worried than normal."

"Oh. I'm just hoping I hid my pouch enough."

"Puh-leeze!" Then Alcie dropped her voice. "It's in a corner of the cave, your toga and robe are on top, and all my stuff is on top of that!"

"And I made sure that the hem of your robe is the first thing anyone would touch because you got a little horse poop on it . . . so, yeah, I guess we're good."

"Okay, didn't know. Thanks for *that* info," Alcie said, then nodded to Pandy's silver tray. "So what have you got?"

"Flatbread points with yogurt and fish eggs, grape leaves stuffed with minced pheasant, and wild boar meatballs. What'd they give you?"

The girls were marching from Chiron's cave toward the palace in a long line of servants, each carrying silver trays of tasty hot and cold tidbits.

"Soup," Alcie said, trying to keep her covered tray steady. "I have lots of tiny bowls of egg-and-lemon soup. And I think I've spilled most of it."

Coming out of a dense thicket on either side of the path, they walked alongside a high wall for many meters, turned to the left, flanked another wall, passed a small bronze plaque that read SERVANT'S ENTRANCE, then finally ascended a wide set of marble stairs to a back terrace.

"Blood oranges!" whispered Alcie.

The enormous white marble palace of King Peleus towered above them, gleaming in the sunlight. There were so many levels Pandy quickly lost count. There were at least thirty terraces and balconies; hundreds of hanging plants; dozens of long porticos; gold tiles on many of the roofs; grassy walkways; brilliantly colored gardens; and fountains and statues featuring heroes, gods, and goddesses everywhere. On this day, every statue was adorned with a laurel wreath, and huge garlands of wildflowers hung over every entrance. As Pandy and Alcie walked along an outer path on the western side, they saw little children wearing crowns of acorns and nuts, standing along a center path with baskets of bread, ready to hand out pieces to the arriving guests as symbols of the offspring Thetis and Peleus would have. In unison, the children were uttering the traditional words, "I fled worse and found better."

Pandy and Alcie entered a small service room being used as a final food staging area. Several warming ovens had been installed with small fires glowing to keep the silver trays warm. Large open chests of ice kept the trays of cold food from souring and spoiling.

Echidna was waiting, standing on a box and shouting to be heard as the room overflowed with servants. She immediately formed all of the temporary servants into groups and delegated responsibility for each group to one of the official palace staff. Pandy and Alcie were fussed with and primped, told to stand straight, smile brightly, and say nothing. Then they were sent with their trays through a series of corridors and into the vast main hall.

"I can't even think of anything to say," Alcie said, stopping for a moment, completely taken aback. Her voice resonated throughout the room. "Zeus's home on Mount Olympus could not have been bigger than this!"

"It was," Pandy replied. "But not by much."

Actually, neither could tell just how big the hall was, because there were flowers everywhere, with the biggest blooms the girls could have imagined. Enormous vases with hundreds of oversized roses and irises were at the four corners of the hall. Special oil lamps had been brought in and filled with garlands of hydrangeas.

Gigantic hyacinths, narcissi, and lilies were intertwined into massive wreaths that hung over every window. Whole cedar trees had been transplanted into pots and placed at various points on the floor, which was not the standard palace white but had been newly retiled in an ocean blue. And there were other flowers blended in that Pandy had never seen before. They looked like they were from another world entirely.

Suddenly, Pandy's left foot collided with something hard, and she nearly went tumbling into Alcie.

"Easy!"

"Sorry, sorry," Pandy said. Then she turned to see what she'd hit and instantly realized it was one leg of Zeus's throne. The very same one she'd seen on Olympus only a few months earlier. Now it was placed at the back of the hall next to Hera's smaller throne so that both would have an unobstructed view of the proceedings. Pandy was about to tell all of this to Alcie when she noticed something else.

"Oh, Gods . . . oh Alcie, look!"

Pandy nodded her head toward the eastern wall.

"No! Grape seeds, you've got to be kidding me!" Alcie said, following Pandy's gaze.

Set on a tiered platform underneath a great bank of open windows were three rows of chairs for the musicians, perhaps twenty in all. The musicians themselves were nowhere to be seen, but their instruments were lying close at hand. There were many lyres of varying sizes, two sets of panpipes, a three-cornered trigonon harp, four bone flutes, a trumpet, and a host of other strange and beautiful musical devices.

But what caught the girls' attention was the oversized chelys lyre with gold accents lying close to the first chair, and a small sign on the floor in front of the platform.

ORPHEUS!
Master of Lyre and Song
and his orchestra
With special guests:
Pan and the Pan-Tones

"Orpheus!" Alcie sighed. "He's just the dreamiest!"

"And we're gonna hear him siiiiiiing! Oh, Alce . . . he is so cute! My dad got two tickets once to hear him in a special concert in front of the Parthenon, but Xander had just been born and Mom didn't want to leave him, so Dad took me! Oh, I almost died!"

"Wait!" Alcie said, confused for a moment. "Pandy . . . *this* is, like, thirteen hundred years before that."

"Yeah, but his mother is Calliope and his father was some sort of Thracian river god. Immortal plus immortal equals immortal. And my father always said that Orpheus was greatest as a rising star, that his early stuff was the best . . . and now we get to hear it *live*!"

Suddenly all of the musicians filed back in from a side terrace. As each began tuning his own instrument, Pandy noted that they all looked bored and rather tired.

"Dad said that musicians are not a happy group," Pandy whispered.

"Hi, Homie!" Alcie called out, seeing Homer behind the wine bar; then she slapped her hand over her mouth. She waved a tiny wave, and Homer waved back.

"You two maidens, quiet . . . now!" said a palace servant in a raised whisper. Then a soft whistle was heard just outside the huge doors at the far end of the hall. One by one, the palace servants answered the whistle. The combined sounds echoed throughout the hall, making the room sound, for just a moment, like an enormous birdcage.

"All right," said the palace servant. "Honored guests are arriving even now. Speak only when spoken to, don't dare to look anyone in the eye, cater to everyone's desires, and appear cheerful at all times or you will be flogged."

The palace servants then placed all of the temporary servants in prime locations around the room. Alcie was told to stand at the back of the hall, close to a terrace exit, and Pandy was placed at the very foot of the grand stairs leading from the hall floor up to the main doors.

Echidna entered from a side hall in heated conversation with a tall, dashing brown-haired man clothed in rich purple and gold and wearing a laurel wreath: "King Peleus," Pandy mused, "the happy groom." Yet, to Pandy, King Peleus seemed agitated, shaking his hands slightly and wiping them on the hem of his golden robe. Echidna began gesturing as if to calm him down, then she finally threw up her hands and said, too sweetly and too loud, "Well, it's a little too late to change the floral color scheme now, Your Highness! And yes, the 'bunches of flowers' as you call them are supposed to be that big . . . they're 'statement displays'! You'll forgive me, Your Highness, but you really should remember: this is *her* day. You're just sort of a delightful . . . ornament, if you will. Excuse me." Then she walked away brusquely, leaving Peleus looking around the hall nervously, reminding Pandy of a little boy lost in a room full of adults. He gazed at the massive floral arrangements, potted trees, garlands, and hanging wreaths, each one more stunning than the last. Finally he plastered a huge smile on his face, then walked over to the center of the room and stood to receive his guests.

A moment after everyone was in place, Echidna, standing at the back of the hall and checking each last detail, gave a nod; two large youths drew back the heavy bolt and opened the doors.

At once, the musicians struck up a delightful background melody and the guests began to enter.

Nymphs, dryads, and naiads began to fill the hall by

the dozens. Next came the remaining seven of the nine muses—gorgeous goddesses of the arts, each an inspiration for a different type of dance, poetry, or song. They were followed by Aeolus, Iris, and Eos. There was a moment's pause, then the three Graces came, almost tumbling, down the stairs: Aglaia (Splendor), Euphrosyne (Mirth), and Thalia (Good Cheer) were literally beside themselves with laughter. Then Pandy saw Hebe, the Goddess of Youth, on the arm of Triton, the Trumpeter of the Sea. She was smiling brightly, although she kept wringing out the sleeve of her robe where it touched the soggy Triton. Persephone came next, followed by Nereus, the Old Man of the Sea, and his wife, Doris. Then Pandy saw Ocean, Lord of the River Ocean, which encircled the earth.

Seeing Ocean, Pandy gasped. She recognized him as a Titan and, therefore, family, although she didn't know exactly where to place him in the family tree.

"But," Pandy thought, "if *he's* here, that means at least some of the Titans were invited. I wonder . . ."

She only had to wonder a split second.

Prometheus came striding through the door, surrounded by the Oceanids, nymphs of the great river . . . all of whom were giggling and flirting madly.

He passed Pandy without a glance.

Her heart dropped out of her chest, until she suddenly remembered she hadn't been born yet. At that moment, she wasn't his daughter; she was just another servant with a plate of wild boar meatballs.

After Prometheus, there was a pause, then a single-file line of stunning young goddesses, dressed exactly alike, slowly entered the hall in perfect step. Each wore an amethyst circlet about her head and a royal purple sash at the waist and each carried an enormous clamshell that contained something dark, dried, and leafy. As they walked they gracefully scattered small handfuls of leaves from side to side. Pandy racked her brain trying to figure out who these women could be. Then she was hit by the acrid, pungent smell wafting from the shells.

Seaweed.

At once, Pandy knew, but just to be certain, she started counting.

"Forty-seven, forty-eight . . . forty-nine . . . and one missing," she thought.

They were Thetis's sisters, the Nereids. Pandy looked at their parents, Nereus and Doris, marveling that Doris had, it was said, bore all fifty of the beautiful sea-nymphs at once.

Suddenly, the strange flowers made sense. And the blue-tiled floor. Thetis, the sea-nymph, and Peleus, the mortal man . . . the whole theme of the wedding was clear: two worlds colliding, a union of earth and sea. The cedar trees meeting the ocean. And Pandy was certain that if she looked closely at the "statement displays," she'd see that the roses, hydrangeas, and hyacinths were mixed with exotic blossoms plucked directly from Poseidon's underwater gardens.

"Wow," she murmured.

In only a matter of minutes, the great hall of the palace of King Peleus was filled with lesser immortals of every shape and size.

Then, after several moments, the music took on a more royal tone and in came the Olympians.

Artemis, Athena, Apollo, Hephaestus, Aphrodite, Poseidon (in a traveling tank, hoisted by several lesser sea-gods), Ares, and a goddess Pandy had not seen when she was on Olympus—Hestia, Goddess of the Hearth—all came strolling in one at a time, to the cheers of those assembled. They were followed shortly afterward by Hermes, helping Dionysus to walk. Pandy marked that the God of Wine had started celebrating way early.

"Like, maybe, last week," she thought. Again, she noticed that Hades was conspicuously absent.

Suddenly, the hall went quiet and every eye turned toward the doors. In a blinding flash of light, Zeus and Hera stepped through the entryway to tremendous applause. Hera, perfect in every way, was smiling like a cat that'd just eaten a lizard, but Zeus's face was a little more somber. With Hera literally clutching his arm, he made his way directly to King Peleus. The king bowed deeply. Zeus looked at Peleus, and Peleus stared back at Zeus.

"Wow. Zeus has to watch the king marry somebody he really cared for," Pandy thought. "Awkward."

"Sky-Lord. Uh," Peleus said.

"Yes," Zeus replied. "Yes. Well, I . . . we . . . wish you every happiness."

"You already said that to Peleus." Hera smiled at her husband.

"I did?" Zeus looked quizzically at Peleus.

"Earlier, Mighty Zeus, at the formal feast," Peleus answered. "But I thank you, again."

"Ah, yes," Zeus said distractedly.

"And how is the bride holding up?" Hera asked, a conspiratorial tone in her voice. "I know when my hubby here and I were married, I was just a shambles! All over the place! I was so scattered, you could have diced me up for gorgon food!"

"Now you tell me," Zeus said. Then he laughed, Peleus laughed, and Hera smiled tightly.

"I assume Thetis is doing well, Queen of Heaven," Peleus replied. "I haven't heard any screaming for a bit, so I think everything is fine. I don't really know. I'm not allowed to see her now until the unveiling."

"Oh, right, right. Quaint mortal custom," Hera said. "Well, I'm off to the wine bar."

Hera turned to walk away.

"Coming, dearest?"

"I shall attend in a moment, light of my life," Zeus said to her without taking his eyes off Peleus. Then softly he said to the king, "She is yours because I trust you, my friend."

"Thank you," Peleus said. "I'll make her a fine husband."

"And she will be a wonderful wife . . . once she calms down."

"ZEEEEEUUUUUSSSS!"

Zeus closed his eyes and sighed.

"My throne arrived?"

"It's waiting for you, Mighty Zeus," Peleus replied.

"Good, because I need to sit."

Then he turned toward Hera.

"Right there, my dove of love."

He walked away, following his wife dejectedly.

CHAPTER SEVEN

The Ceremony

Twenty minutes later, Pandy stepped into the small staging room and found Alcie holding out her tray while a young cook loaded it with more tiny cups of soup.

Alcie tilted her head, indicating that Pandy should meet her outside. After piling more grape leaves and meatballs on her tray, Pandy met Alcie on an adjoining terrace.

"What?" Pandy asked. "Did you see something? A clue? Lust? Did you find it?"

"Apples, no. I just wanted to say, *wow*! These immortals can *eat*!" Alcie said.

"I know! I didn't think the gods ate anything other than ambrosia and nectar," Pandy said. "And you know who eats the most? Aphrodite! She's got the most amazing voice when she talks to you, makes you feel really good, but basically, she's cleaned off my entire tray, like, three times. This is my sixth refill!"

"It's not like she has to exercise," Alcie said. "But how about those tips, huh? I am raking in some serious coinage just for walking around! Who knew? I may have found a new career path."

"And some of it's gold, Alce. I had to wipe yogurt and boar sauce off of my coins, but I'm certain that some of them are pure gold," Pandy said. "Alcie, if this party lasts all night, we could be set for a while, no matter where we go."

"That is, if Echidna doesn't try to take it."

"Oh, I'd like to see her try. Where are you putting yours?"

"Everywhere. Girdle, between my toes, behind my ears," Alcie said.

"Me too, but that's not gonna work after a while," Pandy mused. Thinking fast, she handed Alcie her tray and crept back into the staging room. Taking the covering cloths off two trays of zucchini blossoms stuffed with cracked wheat, she gave one cloth to Alcie and they quickly wrapped their coins in small bundles and hid them behind a stone bench.

"If you find a better hiding place, let me know," Pandy said as the two girls walked back into the storage room.

"*There* are my slackers," Echidna sighed as they entered. She cupped her face in both hands. "You two should have signs over your heads that say 'Just flog me, flog me please . . . I am begging you to flog me.' You have been hired to *serve,* not stand about and chat. The ceremony is about to start. Now get back out there for anyone who wants a last nibble. Then, once Thetis enters the room, I want you both to stand at the top of the stairs just in case any centaurs try to break in and carry off the bride.

"You're so tangerine kidding, *right*?" Alcie choked.

"Excuse me, but how are *we* going to stop centaurs?" Pandy asked. "That's like using a feather to stop a sword."

"You're not supposed to fight them," Echidna said. "You're supposed to distract them. Let them take you instead."

"Like Hades!" Alcie yelled.

"As if!" Pandy yelled at the same time.

"Well, it was all in the contract you signed with the Midas company," Echidna said, pushing them out into the main hall. "So, if you want to be paid and don't want to be flogged . . ."

"I am adding her to the list of things I hate," Alcie whispered as she and Pandy moved into the crowd. "And what's with all the flogging?"

"Look, it's . . . it's not gonna happen," Pandy reassured her, a few notes from Orpheus's lyre catching her ear. "Zeus is here. No centaurs are going to break in. I'll see you in a few."

Alcie headed toward the staircase while Pandy wove

her way across the hall to get an up-close glimpse of Orpheus at work. Pandy recognized the melody he was playing as one her father hummed all the time around the house: "Gimme Goat!" (Also known as "Two Lentils and a String Bean Don't Make a Meal.") Involuntarily, she felt her head bobbing up and down and she put a little dance step into her walk. She caught sight of Alcie, now at the top of the stairs, swaying back and forth with the music. Suddenly, the crowd parted in front of her and Pandy found herself face-to-face with Orpheus (or, as she would call him from then on, the dreamiest man alive in any century). He smiled down at her as he snatched a grape leaf off her tray without missing a beat, and she gurgled. She didn't even care what he was playing. Pandy, although she was very sorry that he'd been turned into a girl, couldn't for the life of her remember what she'd ever seen in Tiresias the Younger.

Without warning, a voice called out from a distance.

"You there! Maiden with the meatballs!"

Pandy had heard Athena speak, and Hephaestus, Apollo, Hermes, and, of course, Zeus. Each had a voice like no other human, or immortal for that matter. Each was its own astonishing combination of characteristics: low, high, soft, harsh, and each was imbued with something Pandy couldn't put her finger on . . . the quality of simply . . . being a god.

But nothing compared with the voice of Aphrodite.

She remembered the few notes she'd heard Apollo pluck on his lyre when she'd stood at the great teardrop table on Mount Olympus. She'd thought then that it was the most beautiful music she'd ever heard. Now, with every call of Aphrodite for more meatballs, all that was changed. Not even the music of Orpheus could compare. This was wind, sun, laughter, pure love, and a sweet cream apricot cake all rolled into one. For no reason at all, Pandy was instantly happy. Pandy felt a subtle ripple in the crowd around her and knew that Aphrodite was headed her way. But the initial tingle of her voice was wearing off and Pandy, now slightly disoriented, retreated a few steps in confusion.

"Meatball maiden!"

There was the tingle again, and Pandy tried to turn toward Aphrodite's voice, but her foot, again, caught on something hard. This time, she went down like a toppled tree; her last glimpse as she hit the floor was of an ornately carved gold throne.

Fortunately, she managed to catch herself before her head smacked the blue tiles, but only because she let the silver tray fly out of her hands. Immediately, the crowd around her parted. Pandy could see meatballs rolling off in every direction. Then she lifted her eyes and, without thinking, looked directly into the scowling face of the Supreme Ruler himself . . . Zeus.

Who was covered with meatballs and boar sauce.

Even the musicians went silent.

With a flick of his finger, Zeus had Pandy on her feet immediately, her tray back in her hand. She was too terrified to say anything. Echidna raced up. Looking at the mess, she heaved for a moment, then turned to Zeus and bowed low.

"I cannot begin to express—," Echidna began, but she was silenced by another flick of Zeus's finger.

"I require music," Zeus said, and Echidna bowed low again and scurried over to Orpheus.

Zeus stared straight at Pandy. Then he picked up a meatball from the arm of his throne and popped it into his mouth.

"Five-second rule," he said.

Pandy almost let her jaw drop but felt it would be decidedly inappropriate, so she hid her lips in a straight line across her face.

As he chewed, Zeus closed his eyes and all the meatballs, on the floor and in his lap, flew out a nearby window, and his robes were gleaming white once again.

Sitting on a smaller throne next to her husband, Hera sneered.

"Mortal."

Zeus gazed at Pandy, but one corner of his mouth turned upward slightly.

"Indeed."

And in that instant, Pandy knew that the chasm of

the centuries didn't matter at all. He knew who she was and why she was there. And she knew it. And he knew that she knew that he knew.

"Approach," he said, and Pandy took two steps closer.

Out of thin air Zeus produced a gold coin, larger and shinier than any other Pandy had seen, and dropped it onto her tray.

"For your service," he said.

Almost at once, the coin was snatched up by two fat fingers.

"I'll just hold on to this for you, my dear, until the evening is through," Echidna said. "All right?"

"It is not," said Zeus evenly.

"But Sky-Lord," Echidna said, forgetting her greed and suddenly terrified, "she has no place to carry such a token. I hold on to all the—"

"She can place it in the pouch at her waist."

The gold coin disappeared out of Echidna's palm, and Pandy felt it secure inside a small red leather pouch now dangling from a cord around her girdle.

"Why . . . uh . . . well, of *course* she can. Silly me," Echidna said.

"Indeed," Zeus replied. Then he paused, and Pandy watched his eyes glaze over for a second, taking him far away.

"Very well," he said with a sigh. "Let's get this over with. Begin."

"I'm not certain that the bride is quite ready, Cloud Gatherer," Echidna said.

"She's ready," Zeus said flatly.

"Absolutely," Echidna replied, and scuttled away toward a purple curtain at the back wall, gesturing frantically at the orchestra. Instantly, a beautiful melody filled the air as a large, round cedar dais was rolled in from a side terrace and set in the middle of the hall. Pandy raced to the staging room and deposited her tray, noticing new red leather pouches on all the servants. She was about to rush back into the main hall when she remembered her and Alcie's tips hidden on the adjoining terrace. Trying to be discreet amidst the servants hurrying about, she snuck outside, swiftly grabbed the bundles from behind the stone bench, and stuffed them into her new pouch. Then she heard a soft sniffle from across the marble flagstones. It was so soft, she wasn't sure at first she'd actually heard anything. But looking down the length of the terrace into the growing darkness, she saw someone standing alone at the far end, hunched over against the railing. Even in the dim light, she knew instantly who it was.

Her father.

But not her father . . . *yet,* she reminded herself.

Without thinking of the consequences to the future, she approached him cautiously.

"Excuse me, sir," she said softly. "Are you all right? May I get you anything?"

"Oh . . . uh . . . no. Thank you, I'm fine. Thank you."

There was the faintest hint of a tremor (which he was attempting to hide) as Prometheus spoke, and even though Pandy could tell that there was something obviously wrong, the sound of her father's voice still made her instantly comfortable.

"Is there anything the matter, sir?"

To him she was only a serving girl, she knew, and still he wouldn't look at her. He stared far off into the darkness.

"Anything the matter?" he echoed. "No. Not really."

Inadvertently, he wiped something from his eye.

Pandy reached into the pouch at her waist and awkwardly dumped the coins from one of the bundles into the pouch, and then she handed the cloth to Prometheus. Finally, he turned, seeing her for the first time. He smiled.

"It's just," he said, dabbing his eyes with the cloth, "that I have always wanted one of these for myself."

"What, sir?" Pandy said.

Prometheus puffed his cheeks and blew the air out slowly.

"Keep a secret?" he said, after a pause.

"Absolutely," Pandy replied.

"A wedding," Prometheus said, straightening up. "A wife, family . . . someone to come home to after a long day of . . . heroic deeds."

Pandy felt closer to her father in that instant than at any other moment of her life. And he was confiding in her, something she knew he didn't do lightly, without knowing who she was . . . or would be.

"Foolish of me, probably."

"I'm sure you'll have that, sir."

"You think so?" he said, smiling.

"I know so," she answered, then realized she may have gone too far.

"Oh, you *know* so, eh?" he said, looking at her, amused.

"Well," Pandy said, choosing her words carefully, "I think there must certainly be someone out there who will be just right for you, sir. And she'll be beautiful. Really beautiful. Like, scary beautiful. And then you'll have the family you want."

"Scary beautiful? All right then. I'll be on the lookout," he said, leaning his back against the railing. "And thank you for that vote of confidence; I will take it to heart. Now, if you wouldn't mind keeping the fact that I was crying like an old woman to yourself, I'd be grateful."

"It will be our secret, sir."

From inside the palace, there was a loud call of a trumpet.

"I guess they're starting," Prometheus said.

"Yes," Pandy replied. "I need to take my place."

"See you later," he said.

"Yes, you will. I mean, uh, I hope so, sir."

Prometheus looked at her as if she were both odd and amusing, then walked into the staging area and disappeared into the hall.

"You don't how right you are," Pandy thought. "I will most definitely see you later!"

She rushed back into the throng of guests and headed toward the staircase, where Alcie was already waiting. Reaching the top, she motioned Alcie over to the back wall near the doors.

"Have something for you," Pandy whispered.

She pulled out the remaining bundle of coins and handed it to Alcie.

"Here."

"Where'd you get that?" Alcie asked softly, looking at the pouch.

"You have one, too. All the servants do now. They were a gift from Zeus when Echidna tried to take his tip from me."

Alcie looked at her waist: sure enough, there was a red pouch dangling from a cord. She untied the bundle and looked at the coins.

"Wrong cloth," Alcie said, handing it back to Pandy. "I had some funky-looking coins that had words like

'Cyprus' and 'Kythira' engraved on them and they're not here."

"Oh, Ares' beard," Pandy muttered. "Like it really matters."

"I'm just sayin'."

Pandy emptied her pouch into her hand and handed all the coins to Alcie.

"Okay. Satisfied?"

"Yes," Alcie said calmly. "Except this one is yours. Because I'm honest."

Alcie handed Zeus's oversized gold coin back to Pandy, who was about to put it back into her pouch when she looked at it closely. The words MOUNT IDA were engraved on one side, and LOSE TWO WEEKS on the other.

"What does that mean?" asked Alcie.

Suddenly there was another loud blast of the trumpet and the crowd quieted, waiting. Pandy and Alcie moved into a better position and tried to look ceremonial. From their vantage point, they could see everything and watched King Peleus and Thetis's father, Nereus, step onto the dais with great formality. Peleus acknowledged all assembled with a nod of his head. Then the music stopped and all eyes turned toward the purple curtain, now being slowly drawn aside.

Then the curtain stopped.

"Unh . . . wait!" screeched a female voice.

"Move!" yelled someone else.

The curtain began to move again.

Suddenly a loud wail shot though the hall.

Everyone turned to look at King Peleus, who chuckled graciously to the crowd, then cleared his throat, wringing his hands behind his back.

The children Pandy had seen on the main walkway with baskets of bread appeared again, this time with jars of white orchid petals. As the crowd parted, they created a white runner leading past Zeus and Hera, on toward the dais.

Euterpe stepped through the curtain, walking slowly and elegantly. Calliope followed several meters behind her. Then Demeter appeared with Iole holding her long hair of summer wheat. Within only seconds, Demeter's hair changed to autumn leaves, which fell amongst the orchid petals, leaving Iole with nothing to hold. Then Demeter's hair became winter icicles and Iole found herself sloshing through petal-filled puddles. Instantly, these dried as Demeter's hair grew into green spring tendrils, and Iole rushed to catch her hair once again.

As all three goddesses took their place around the dais, the four nymphs who had been dressing and styling the bride stepped through the curtain and into the hall.

Then Thetis, her lips pursed but her head held high and her eyes staring straight ahead, walked into the room. She was resplendent in her gold gown and robes, her hair piled high on her head and studded with rubies and pearls, matching the gems on her long, slender neck. But no sooner had she appeared in the entryway than, before anyone could get a look at her face, the four nymphs dissolved into a gold mist, swirled about Thetis for an instant, then settled over her hair and face, creating an exquisite golden veil and giving Thetis a golden glow. Even Zeus gasped as spontaneous applause broke out among the guests.

Walking forward, Thetis acknowledged her reception through the veil, nodding to as many of the immortals as she could. Then she spied Zeus on his throne, and her step faltered. Zeus bit his lip and furrowed his brow, subtly jerking his head toward the dais. Within moments, a soft sobbing could be heard underneath the golden shimmer.

"That's right, sweetheart. Cry those pretty tears, but keep walking," Hera muttered.

With another flick of his finger, Zeus moved Thetis forward quickly until she reached her father and her waiting groom. As she stepped up onto the dais, the musicians ended their melody and the crowd was hushed once again. Iole, so close to the proceedings, was fascinated by the unfolding, symbolic drama. But Thetis's sobbing was slightly more than symbolic, and an uncomfortable tension began to build until Zeus, unseen by anyone, silenced the bride once and for all. Peleus just stood in front of Thetis, awestruck at her beauty, even hidden by a veil, until Nereus prodded him with his elbow.

"Oh!" Peleus said. "Right . . . right."

He grabbed Thetis's wrist to show to all assembled that she was now his "property," while Nereus said the traditional words:

"In front of witnesses, I give this girl to you."

Hera coughed loudly.

"And it's about time," she said under her breath.

Pandy and Alcie reached for each other's hands. This was *the* moment, the one every other aspect of the ceremony had been leading up to . . . the formal unveiling; Peleus would look upon Thetis for the first time as his wife.

Pandy squeezed Alcie's hand tightly. A hush fell over the crowd as everyone held their breath and guests strained over one another to get a first glimpse of the bride. Peleus reached for the hem of the shimmering veil and as he did, a single nymph broke from the bottom of the mist and soared overhead, regaining her own form.

The crowd gasped in delight and Peleus reached forward again.

Without warning, the hall was rocked by a huge crash as something enormous hit the wooden doors behind

Pandy and Alcie. It was so loud that several immortals screamed as everyone turned to look. Another crash followed quickly; the bolt held firm but the left door was beginning to crack and splinter.

"Centaurs!" Alcie cried.

But Pandy knew in a flash that it wasn't centaurs. She had been so caught up in the spirit and beauty of the celebration that she had all but forgotten the major twist in this famous wedding. The horrible event.

"Get away from the doors," Pandy said, pushing Alcie behind her.

Zeus nodded to Hermes, standing beside his father's throne, and instantly Hermes materialized at the top of the stairs . . . only a second too late. A third crash blew open the doors, sending one door straight into Hermes, knocking him aside, before it careened down the staircase. The other hurtled high into the air; where, and on whom, it would have landed was anyone's guess, had not Zeus slowly lowered it to lean against the wine bar.

A woman stood in the entryway engulfed in a deep crimson light and thick smoke. Stepping out of the billows, she picked her way gingerly over Hermes, walking to the edge of the stairs to address the astonished guests in a high, delicate voice.

"Did I miss anything?"

CHAPTER EIGHT

Eris

"You must forgive my rather loud entrance," the woman said sweetly, "but the doors . . . well, I think they were *barred*!"

Pandy, trying to hide with Alcie and several other servants behind the curving banister of the staircase, took note of the woman's mismatched robes and the odd colors woven throughout the messy rat's nest of her hair.

"I am so sorry to be late, but my invitation arrived only . . . only . . . gosh, now that I think of it . . ."

For a moment, the woman's voice turned hard and cold.

". . . *it never arrived at all!* Why is that, I wonder?"

Peleus sprang from the dais and strode swiftly across the hall at the same moment that Hermes was on his feet again.

"Perhaps it is still at the stonecutters, hmmm?" she said, now smiling.

Pandy looked across the hall at Zeus, who was sitting motionless, his mouth a grim line as he watched the woman. Then Pandy caught Iole's stare as she stood next to the dais. Iole was on alert. This had to be why they were here.

"Perhaps the runner lost his way to my home? Hmmm?"

Hermes was now standing directly in front of the woman only two steps below. Peleus, Prometheus, Hephaestus, and Apollo had formed a line at the bottom of the stairs. Pandy noticed that Ares, standing close to the other gods, had not joined them but was, instead, smiling broadly at his sister.

"At any rate, I'm here . . . *now!*" the woman said, spreading her arms wide. "Let the fun begin!"

"You are not wanted here, Eris," Hermes said, his voice low and threatening.

Behind Pandy, several servants gasped.

Eris, the Goddess of Discord, squared her shoulders and smiled even brighter.

"Out of my way, errand boy," she said sweetly, but with an edge. "I've come to pay my respects to the bride and groom."

"Leave my house," Peleus called from the bottom of the stairs. Eris met his glare for a moment before sighing.

"What a tone to take with an immortal," she giggled.

Pandy was suddenly aware of raised voices in several areas around the hall.

"Eris needs to go!"

"Don't tell me I've had too much to drink!"

"Well, I think she should stay!"

"What do you mean I look fat?"

"I never liked your mother!"

Quarrels and disagreements began popping up everywhere as strife erupted throughout the room. Eris looked across the hall to Thetis.

"I'm certain the bride would like me here, wouldn't you, my friend?"

Thetis, still hidden under her veil, gasped and reached for her father's arm. Pandy looked for Iole but she was nowhere to be seen. In one corner of the hall, someone shouted an expletive. In another, a wine goblet clattered to the floor. In a small cluster of Thetis's sisters, someone actually shoved someone else into a floral display. Then a voice boomed out above the growing commotion.

"Eris."

At once the hall quieted down and all eyes turned toward the golden throne.

"Should you manage to get past Hermes," Zeus said calmly, after a pause, "which is highly unlikely, and should you succeed in circumventing the formidable barricade at the bottom of the stairs, you would then, sweeting, have to deal with me. And I can promise you that I shall make those following moments a study in agony that will seem to last an eternity. And it just might. Now, dear one, do you really want that?"

Eris's smile faltered slightly and her hands began to tremble with rage, but her eyes stayed on Zeus.

"You were not invited to this wedding for the same reason you are not invited to any other. No one wants discord and strife on such joyous occasions. I'm terribly sorry your feelings are hurt, but I'm certain you can find a tavern or a schoolyard or gambling house and work a little mischief to make you feel better. So now, and I will not say it again, be gone!"

Pandy glanced at Ares, now looking rather somber. Of course Ares only concerned himself with great battles, whole countries in conflict; he would never use his powers on something as insignificant as a wedding. "But," Pandy thought, "Discord was the younger, more benign sibling of War, and Ares probably wanted Eris to stay just to have someone with the same interests to talk to."

The great hall was silent for several seconds. Then Eris licked her lips and, with a tiny snort, pointedly shifted her gaze from Zeus to the guests.

"Well!" she sang out, her words now very crisp. "Of course I didn't really want to *stay*. I just *can't*, you see . . . so much else to do. Very full schedule. I just wanted to congratulate the happy couple, and now that I have done that, I'm afraid I really must be off."

She paused, looking around the room, her head cocked slightly as if she were deep in thought. Then she smiled again and, turning, walked swiftly from the hall.

At once, calm settled back into the room, and Pandy heard a few "I'm sorry's" from several guests close by.

"Hephaestus?" called Zeus.

"My lord?" Hephaestus called back.

"How long to fix the doors?"

Hephaestus looked at the wooden doors and stroked his beard.

"Five ticks of a sundial, maybe less."

"Do so," said Zeus, and Hephaestus and the doors disappeared. "Apollo, Ares, Hermes, and Prometheus, guard the entryway."

In a flash, the four immortals raced up the stairway and blocked the opening, facing inward so as not to miss the proceedings. As he settled, Prometheus happened to notice Pandy and winked in recognition. Pandy glanced at Hermes, who stared at her knowingly for an instant. Iole hurried up the stairs and slid in next to Pandy.

"So exciting!" she gushed. "We're seeing just how it all really happened!"

"So now what?" Alcie said. "Eris is a bit of a wacko, but I didn't see any Lust anywhere. What do we do?"

"Athena's toenails! You really *didn't* pay attention in class, did you?" Pandy said.

"Kumquats, so kill me already!"

"Just watch," Iole said.

Peleus was making his way back to the dais, where Thetis waited. As he stepped up, Thetis took his hand and whispered, "You were very heroic." Then she leaned close to his face, softly cooing, "I am so proud of you . . . *my husband,*" giving his fingers a tiny squeeze. Peleus genuinely smiled for the first time in two days and quickly reached for the second segment of her golden veil. As before, the mist dissolved and the nymph floated high above in her true shape. Thetis began to laugh softly, as did Peleus, and the third segment of the veil was dissipated quickly. Now only one remained, covering her face just below her mouth.

As he slowly reached for it, Pandy glanced behind her, beyond the massive legs of Ares and Hermes and out through the entryway. Eris was nowhere to be seen, but for a split second, Pandy thought she caught a faint reddish glow in the treetops on the hillside below the formal gardens. The oohs and aahs of the guests made her turn quickly. Peleus had barely touched the mist and it dissolved so fast that he was almost shocked to see Thetis's beautiful face smiling brightly before him. As the cheers, shouts, and applause rang out (Hera forced Zeus to clap) and Peleus bent to kiss his now willing bride, Pandy had an overwhelming urge to turn again toward the gardens. Amongst the low-lying flowers and strewn rose petals, her eyes caught no movement at first . . .

. . . and then she saw it.

A small red ball was rolling up the main path, toward the entryway. Slow at first, it was picking up speed with every moment, and as the joyous commotion in the hall reached its zenith, Pandy grabbed Alcie's and Iole's arms and they turned immediately to see the red ball hurtling toward them. Faster and faster the ball was rolling, now only several meters away. In the doorway, Prometheus looked down at the three serving girls, all of whom were looking in the opposite direction from the scene in the hall. As he whipped his head around, Hermes caught his movement and both immortals saw the red ball now almost airborne along the path.

Hermes and Prometheus closed their feet together, trying to stop it, but they were too late and the ball flew past them in a red blur. Apollo and Hermes shouted warnings at the same time as the ball raced down the stairs. Immortals panicked and hurried out of its way, tripping and falling over each other. Peleus instinctively stepped in front of his bride as several of her sisters began screaming, but the ball was moving in another direction. It swerved and dodged, rolling this way, then that, at lightning speed, almost with a mind of its own, until finally it came to a sudden and full stop at the feet of Athena . . . who did not flinch.

Immediately, everyone backed away to form a large circle around her as all eyes were trained on the ball. When nothing happened after several moments, Athena huffed and bent slowly to pick it up. Before she could touch it, the ball began to tremble slightly, then shake; then steam began to rush out from a crack that had split one side. Several guests fell back, grasping each other's arms; others clutched their own garments, gasping loudly. Lifting her enormous sword, Athena aimed the point at the ball. Suddenly, as quickly as it had begun, the shaking stopped and the steam disappeared. The crack split wider and the ball fell to pieces, revealing a bright flash. Even those who couldn't see clearly heard the loud *thunk* as an object enclosed inside the ball hit the blue tiles and rolled in a lazy arc, coming to rest against the tip of Athena's blade.

And everyone stared down at the small, perfect, golden . . .

. . . apple.

CHAPTER NINE
"To The..."

"Gods. Prunes!" Alcie whispered. "Where have I been?"

"Meaning?" Iole said. The girls stood at the staircase railing, watching the crowd stare down at the apple.

"I had clues in front of me this entire time. I gotta start thinking more," Alcie answered quietly. "This is *that* wedding. Even if I wasn't paying attention in class, I know enough to know about that . . . *this* . . . wedding."

She was trying to get another glimpse of the golden fruit as Athena, her brows furrowed, rolled it to and fro with her sword.

"So," Iole said, arching one eyebrow, "you're all caught up now?"

"Fully informed, thank you very much."

"Pandy, what do we do?" Iole asked.

Pandy was silent. She knew what was about to happen, but she still didn't know exactly where Lust was hiding—if it was even in the room. Yet, looking at her friends, she realized that she felt incredibly ineffectual. For hours, all she or any of them had been doing was observing and looking for clues. She'd taken no serious action of any kind. With great effort she reminded herself that this was not the moment to spring, that biding their time was all that they could do until they were certain of something, anything, but she'd never felt so . . . bound . . . in her life.

"We let it play out," she sighed, staring across the hall into the middle of the crowd. "Watch."

Athena bent and swiftly scooped up the apple. Holding it by the tiny golden stem, she twirled it slowly in front of her. She stopped, suddenly noticing something, and out of nowhere, a delicate smile appeared on her face.

"What's that on the side?" Ares called to her.

"Nothing," Athena said softly, hiding the apple from view with her hand. "It's nothing."

"Something's written on it," Hebe said, standing close by.

"Athena," said Triton from across the wide circle, "what does it say?"

Athena, as if she never wanted to look anywhere but at the apple, tore her gaze away and looked at Triton, still smiling.

"It says, 'To The Fairest.'"

"Here we go," Pandy murmured.

"Excuse me! Pardon me! Step to the left, if you would . . . thank you very much. Pardon me!"

Aphrodite's voice sounded like wind chimes as it carried throughout the hall. From her vantage point, Pandy saw a ripple in the crowd and flashes of white and rose-colored robes as Aphrodite began to move toward Athena.

At the back of the hall, Pandy caught a whirl of blue as Hera rose up off her throne, her arms waving madly as she yelled something toward Zeus. As Hera began to stride toward Athena, rolling up the sleeves of her deep cerulean robes, her words became audible.

"You better *not* have gotten that for her," she called back over her shoulder. "Getting her married off was present enough!"

"It is not my doing, my stuffed grape leaf of love," Zeus said as he watched his wife hurry away. Unlike Aphrodite's insistent but gentle parting of the throng, Hera was actually sending guests flying into walls and floral displays if they didn't get out of her path fast enough.

"I don't care if your power *is* greater than all the rest of us combined, husband," she was yelling to herself. "I will kick your big and powerful butt!"

Pandy, Alcie, and Iole watched the two goddesses move through the hall. Hera arrived first at Athena's side.

"For the fairest? I'll just take that, if you don't mind, dearest," she said, making a quick grab for the apple.

But Athena was too swift and dropped the apple into her palm. Pandy saw that the moment her hand closed around the apple, Athena's knuckles went white and her body tensed.

"With all respect due to you, Queen of Heaven," Athena said, holding the apple high. "I don't think so."

"Hear me, Gray Eyes—"

"Of course you wouldn't give it to her," Aphrodite said, gliding up. "It says 'To The Fairest,' and I think we all can agree on who that—"

"You would *disobey* the wife of Zeus? Acknowledged as the most beautiful of all the immortals?"

"Right, well, we all know *that's* not true. Give me the apple, Theeny," said Aphrodite.

"Alpha, I'd disobey you in a heartbeat," said Athena, glaring at Hera, "because you're not going to do anything about it, and beta, this is obviously meant for me . . ."

"Me!" Aphrodite said.

"Me, you shield-wielding savage!"

". . . because it rolled right to me!"

"*You* are not the fairest!" spat Hera.

"It landed *at my feet*!" Athena screamed. "That means it's supposed to be for—"

"You don't even look right in a *gown* with that silly sword!"

"Hellooo!" Aphrodite called out. "Goddess of Love and BEAUTY! Right here!"

And while Athena was distracted, still arguing with Hera, Aphrodite reached up and snatched the apple out of Athena's hand. As her flesh touched the golden fruit, Aphrodite lurched forward in an ungainly way, a gasp escaping her lips. Before anyone could even blink, the tip of Athena's sword sliced neatly between two strands of Aphrodite's twelve-strand necklace of perfectly matched pearls and pressed not so lightly into the flawless white skin of Aphrodite's throat.

"Theeny, you wouldn't!" Aphrodite gasped.

"Try me."

"Give me . . . *that,*" Hera growled as she viciously snatched the apple away from Aphrodite. Grasping it, Hera let out a truly ungoddesslike yelp as her body shook once, violently. Athena redirected her blade at Hera as Aphrodite slapped at Athena's arms.

"Heeeey!" came a loud screech from the main wine bar.

The crowd quickly parted to reveal Dionysus lying on his stomach on top of the bar, his head turned toward the fracas. His lips were pushed out as his face mashed into the wooden bar top.

"Anyone even consider actually giving it to the— *uuurrrrrppp*—excuse me, bride?"

The three goddesses gaped at him with blank

expressions for a moment, then broke into a simultaneous derisive laugh and went at one another again as the wedding guests watched in astonishment.

Suddenly, as she and Aphrodite were flailing about like children, trying to grab the apple from Hera, Athena paused.

"Listen . . . listen!" She wheezed ever so slightly. "I have an idea."

"What is it, you big bully?" Aphrodite said.

"We shall allow the assembled populace to decide."

"Who?" asked Hera.

"The guests, you goat!" said Athena. "We'll do it the mortal way. We'll all take a vote."

"All right," said Hera after a moment.

"Goody," said Aphrodite, taking a quick count of all of her suitors and lovers in the room. "I'm a shoo-in."

The first immortal Athena grabbed was Ocean. As the three goddesses stood before him, Hera began winking wildly, Aphrodite puffed out her stomach to make her magic girdle (known for its seductive powers) a focal point, and Athena rested both hands on the hilt of her sword.

"Choose!" said Hera.

Ocean looked, blindsided and terrified, from one to the next to the last.

"You have got to be k-k-kidding!" he finally stammered.

Then he dissolved into a saltwater puddle, which flowed toward the nearest exit.

"Uncle!" cried Athena, watching Poseidon rushing his tank-bearers toward the stairs.

"Not a chance!"

"Why not?" Aphrodite called out.

"And risk the wrath of the other two?" Poseidon answered. "I'd rather look into the eyes of Medusa!"

"Ouch," Alcie muttered.

"Can't take it personally, Alce," Iole said. "You haven't been born yet, and he doesn't know Medusa is your aunt."

"Right. Not personal. Right. Still kinda tacky, though, right, Pandy?"

But Pandy was watching the goddesses as they chased after the guests, many of whom were heading slyly and slowly for the exits. They had fallen upon the God of Wine, still lying on top of the bar.

"Pick one, you besotted lout!" Hera yelled, digging her finger into his side.

"All right!" Dionysus mumbled. "All right. Stop poking. I'll pick one!"

There was silence as everyone close by held their breath.

"I think the fairest is," he slurred, raising his goblet full of crimson liquid, "the *red!* See? The wine!"

Athena moved to strike him with the flat edge of her sword, but Dionysus, with a smelly belch, fell backward off the bar.

"Look at Athena," Pandy said.

"Why?" said Iole.

"The other two . . . I get it. Of course Aphrodite would think the apple is for her. And Hera's ego is the size of Egypt, so no big mystery there. But Athena is too wise to let something like this go to her head. And she knows . . . she knows . . . she's not, like, the super, all-time, *woo-woo* fairest. But then she touched it!"

At that moment, Hephaestus appeared with the newly repaired doors and began pounding behind them.

"So, it's the apple?" Alcie said, cupping her hands around her mouth to be heard.

"It has to be. Aphrodite and Hera . . . you saw them; they felt its effects as soon as they got it. And did you see how Athena's face changed when she held it? She is always so serious and . . . and . . ."

"Tense, resolute, reserved, decorous . . . grave?" Iole offered.

"Yep," Pandy agreed loudly. "But holding the apple, she glowed."

"So we go get it," Alcie said.

But Pandy hesitated.

Suddenly a cry went up from Thetis. Pandy couldn't hear exactly what she was saying, but she was gesturing to the departing crowd, Hephaestus hammering away, and the three goddesses racing all over the hall. She fell sobbing into Peleus's shoulder.

"ENOUGH!"

Those guests still in the hall stood stock-still.

Zeus was off his throne and walking toward Athena, Hera, and Aphrodite.

"This has gone on long enough!" he bellowed. "Everyone . . . attend!"

In an instant, all the guests who had managed to escape were back in the hall, including Ocean, dripping wet.

"This was mildly amusing for about two ticks of a sundial. Now the three of you are displaying as much selfishness and self-centeredness as I could stomach for the rest of eternity. Aphrodite . . . well, never mind."

Aphrodite only smiled.

Then Zeus turned on Hera.

"You, wife. I expected better of you. But then, I always do and I am always disappointed."

"Oh!" Hera sniffed.

"But Athena. You of whom I am most proud. What has become of my daughter? To be reduced to this . . . begging for favor, scrabbling about, threatening your family?"

"I don't know," Athena said slowly, kicking at the floor. "I just want it. Is that so wrong?"

"It is when you ruin everything around you," Zeus said, glowering. Pandy flashed back to the first time she saw that glower, when it was directed right at her as she stood facing Zeus for the first time.

"Let me put it this way . . . and I'll use a term that will gain popularity many centuries from now: 'You're bringing down the room.' "

Many immortals looked suspiciously at the ceiling.

"I *mean*," Zeus said with exasperation, "that you are spoiling the festivities. Destroying everyone's good time. Forcing friends and family to make a decision that is impossible. You are all three the fairest in your own way, and your lack of confidence astounds me. Especially you, Athena . . . and you, Aphrodite. Hera . . . all right . . . not so much. But don't the three of you think it's odd that this apple appeared after Eris was banned from attending? Perhaps this might have something to do with her? A trick of some sort, a bit of cold revenge. Did that not occur to *you*, at least, Athena?"

"Maybe," she mumbled, "but I don't care."

She glanced sideways at Hera, who, somehow, had gained possession of the apple, and whacked Hera's bottom with her sword, sending the blue-robed goddess sprawling with a yelp onto the tiles. Immediately Aphrodite was on top of Hera, grappling for the shiny piece of fruit. Then Athena jumped onto Aphrodite, creating a goddess dog pile. Almost instantly they began to roll around the floor in a screeching ball of fabric and flying limbs, scratching, clawing, biting, and kicking.

"THAT'S *IT*!" yelled Zeus, and now a little dust *did* fall from the ceiling as some of the timbers and stones began to loosen slightly.

At the sound of his voice, the three goddesses found themselves at opposite points in the room, guests scattering away from them.

"I had hoped that reason and good sense would prevail, or at the very least, good manners. That whatever enchantment of desire Eris has put on this foul thing . . ."

And at this point, attempting to disguise it as a display of disgust, Zeus shifted his gaze ever so slightly in Pandy's direction.

"I get it," Pandy thought.

". . . might not affect you, as immortals, as shamefully and revoltingly as it has. But I can see that I was wrong."

Zeus strode to the middle of the room and gazed at each goddess in turn.

"You will, together, leave this place at once. I am giving you one day from this moment to prepare yourselves as you will. Don your finest robes; adorn yourselves with your costliest jewels. Hera, my little swan, you might want to moisturize. Since this inane contest is so important to you, you will have your answer. But we will allow . . . a mortal to decide."

Smiling, Aphrodite quickly totaled up the number of mortal lovers and suitors she'd known and thought, again, that she was a shoo-in. Athena and Hera both opened their mouths to protest. But a look from Zeus silenced them.

"We will need someone young; someone with little to lose and naive enough not to know the danger in which he'll be. Someone several arrows short of a full quiver. Fortunately, I know just the boy. You will go together, with Hermes as your escort, to Mount Ida in Phrygia and find the shepherd named Paris. It shouldn't be too hard . . . he'll be the one who's dressed the surrounding trees and several of his flock to resemble residents of his village. He'll probably be yelling at them for moving too slow . . . trying to dance with them or some such nonsense. Aphrodite, for the life of me I don't know why, but in this instance I trust you to safeguard the apple until then."

"Not fair!" Athena yelled.

"QUIET!" Zeus bellowed.

Pandy felt her stomach flip at the sheer size of his voice. Zeus paused for a moment, his brows suddenly furrowed.

"If two relatively sane immortals and my wife are so ridiculous over this bauble, I suffer to think what its power would do to a human. Therefore, to mitigate the destructive power of Eris's spell, I am enchanting the apple with an invisible shield," he said when he spoke again. "Which will be broken only when one of you receives it in your big, greedy hands. Give it to Paris and let him judge."

At once, Aphrodite felt the apple heavy in a silver silk pouch hanging from a new hook on her enchanted girdle.

"Well," Zeus said, when no one moved. "What are you three waiting for? Time is ticking . . . and some of you need all of it you can get."

Athena and Aphrodite vanished straightaway, but Hera shot one last look at her husband, murmuring something inaudible, and then she was gone.

"Blah, blah, blah," Zeus said softly. His gaze went to Thetis, who mouthed the words "thank you." Zeus nodded his head, then he swept his arms wide to include all the guests.

"Well, the boy is in for it, I'm certain, but at least we've avoided our own little war, yes?"

The immortals cheered.

"And the best part of all is that now I may have one dance with the bride without my wife wanting to peck out my eyes!"

To which everyone laughed and agreed.

"That is, of course, if her husband will permit me?"

King Peleus bowed low and assisted Thetis off the dais. The new queen did not go rushing into Zeus's arms as she might have only several hours before, like an infatuated schoolgirl. Instead, she walked slowly and regally, mindful of her husband's feelings, to the Sky-Lord.

"Friends?" Zeus asked her.

"Always," she answered.

"Orpheus?" Zeus called out. "How about something with a little kick?"

"At once, Cloud Gatherer!" Orpheus cried, then softly to his orchestra, "Boys, 'I Found Love in a Syrian Spice Shop' on three. A one, a two . . ."

Soon almost everyone was out on the floor, feet stomping and arms waving.

But Pandy was slumped over the railing at the top of the stairs, her mouth slightly open . . . in complete and utter shock.

CHAPTER TEN

Departure

Pandy stared blankly at the guests, celebrating madly in the great hall. By now, she thought, she should be used to this particular feeling . . . she'd felt it so many times before: she was completely at a loss.

"Pandy?"

Iole was nudging her, but Pandy was oblivious. It had been so *close,* right in the room, only several meters away: the golden apple that was Lust . . . or contained it . . . or led to it. And she'd done nothing. She could have quietly tiptoed up behind any of the three most powerful goddesses in the universe and tried to take it. It shouldn't have mattered that they would have killed her on the spot. She could have kicked them or tickled them or pointed in another direction, grabbed it, and raced out of the room when they weren't looking or . . .

"Pandy!"

Alcie was pinching her arm, but she didn't care. The

entire day had been a series of "watch" or "look" or, worst of all, "wait." Not one single "run!" or "go!" She was disgusted with herself.

And now the golden apple was gone. Vanished with Aphrodite and the others to someplace called Mount Ida in Phrygia, which was no place in Greece, that much she knew. But it was of no consequence to Zeus where he sent them; he could have told the three quarreling goddesses to go to China and it would still be the same to Pandy—too far for three mortal maidens and a youth to travel in the single day before the shepherd would choose.

"Pandy!"

Alcie had her by the shoulders and was shaking her forcefully.

"Hey!"

"What? What!" Pandy said.

"What do we do now?" Alcie asked as Iole came around to join them. Pandy had no earthly idea what they were going to do.

"I . . . I . . ."

"That *was* it, wasn't it? Lust?" Iole asked.

She put her head in her hands, unsure if this was a question she could even deal with. Just when she thought she might pass out, a voice deep inside her head screamed, "Knock it off, Pandora. You're in charge, remember?" She lifted her head and forced her mouth open.

"It . . . has . . . to be. Right?" she began slowly and uncertainly, but almost at once, her brain miraculously found a thread and she ran with it. "Okay. We were sent here *today*. Not yesterday, not tomorrow. Not earlier and not later. *Now*. We were meant to see everything that just happened. So . . . so, look around . . . " There was that inactive word again, but this time she said it for a specific purpose. "Do you see anything that resembles Lust anywhere? No. Nowhere. Even Peleus and Thetis . . . they look happy, but not crazy. Not Athena-crazy."

"But Lust is going to Mount Ida," said Iole.

"Why does that sound familiar?" asked Alcie, her eyes gazing at three nymphs flinging their arms out to their sides with the beat of the music.

"Aphrodite is probably back on Olympus right now, preparing," Pandy said, grasping for something hopeful. "That's still in Greece, at least. If Alcie and I pooled our tips, we could get the . . . the swiftest chariot."

"Even if we could travel there in a day, no ordinary chariot could ever get up the slopes of Olympus," Iole countered. "We have to get to Mount Ida."

"I've heard that name before," Alcie said, her brow furrowing slightly.

"Right, Mount Ida," Pandy said, a measure of authority creeping into her voice.

"Phrygia is to the east," Iole said. "It's fairly close to Troy, but it's across the sea."

"Okay," Pandy said, staring at her. "So we're in the same spot that we were in Alexandria . . ."

"Gods!" Alcie yelled. Several immortals close by looked at her as if she had summoned them all at once, but Pandy was too engrossed in her own words to notice.

". . . except now we have to get to Mount Ida," Pandy continued. "There's no Sun Chariot to take us."

"I don't think we need it," said Alcie, unusually quiet, grinning from ear to ear.

"No dolphins," Pandy went on.

"Pandy, we couldn't even depart Mount Pelion in a day," Iole said.

"Oh, lemons," Alcie said softly. "Guys, I, like, so don't get to do this that often, please just listen to me."

"Huh?" Pandy said. "Do what, Alce?"

"Be smart."

"What are you talking about?" Iole asked.

"Pandy," Alcie said, folding her arms across her chest. "*Look* in your red pouch."

"Why?" Pandy asked, looking from Alcie down to her waist. Then she looked back up at Alcie, her eyes wide.

"Gods!" Pandy cried. Several immortals turned to glare at the girls, but Pandy stared at Alcie, who just nodded, smiling. Pandy ripped open the pouch and poured the coins into her hand. There, on top, was the large gold coin from Zeus with the words MOUNT IDA just readable in the fading afternoon light.

"You're brilliant," Pandy said to Alcie.

"I have moments."

"Are you certain that's not simply where it was stamped?" Iole said, never having seen the coin before.

"I'm certain," Pandy said. "Look what it says on the back."

Pandy flipped the coin over.

"We'll lose two weeks of time, but my guess is that this will get us all there tomorrow . . . or instantly whenever we use it."

"And when do we use it?" Iole said. "Or more specifically, how? And where?"

Pandy glanced about the room, again at a loss, but this time confident that something would present itself.

"We know that the gods don't do anything without a reason, and this came from Zeus himself. We'll know it when we see it."

"Or when I think of it," Alcie said.

"Don't get cocky," Iole replied, rolling her eyes.

"Can if I want to!" Alcie sang out, poking at the air in front of Iole.

"Come on, let's get back to the cave and get our stuff," Pandy said.

"Everything of mine is in the bride's dressing room," Iole answered.

"Okay," Pandy said, "we'll get Homer on our way out. You meet us at the fork in the path to Chiron's cave in ten minutes."

"Done."

Iole split off and headed toward the purple curtain as Pandy and Alcie headed in the direction of the main wine bar, all three completely unaware that two beady eyes, lids painted with pale green shadow, were watching their every move.

Leaving Homer at the fork to wait for Iole, Pandy and Alcie walked past many large ox-drawn carts, each being loaded with sacks of garbage from the evening's festivities.

Suddenly Pandy grabbed Alcie's arm.

"What?"

"It just hit me," Pandy said, turning slowly to look at her friend. "Zeus *gave* me the coin. That means he doesn't just know that I'm here and why I'm here, but that he's helping as well. Hermes *and* Zeus!"

"Uh-huh," Alcie said, as if she'd already figured that out. "I don't know about you, but I'm gonna take that as a good sign. C'mon."

Inside Chiron's cave, there was almost no activity

except for a few servants cleaning up and carrying sacks out to the waiting carts. Walking to the spot where they had put their cloaks and pouches, they stopped when they heard a high-pitched laugh followed by a deep guffaw.

At the back of the cave, Myron and Chiron were sitting, one on his haunches, the other at a table, laughing uproariously. Suddenly Chiron sighed, and Myron became very solemn.

"Look, Horsey, here's the thing," Myron said. "We can joke about it all we want, but it's resentment, pure and simple. Just because you didn't get an invitation . . . doesn't mean a thing. We're better than just about everybody we serve. Artistes, that's what we are! I cook, you teach . . . and look great. And do we ever get the recognition we deserve?"

"Nope," Chiron answered.

"The answer is no. You should have been there tonight. I fed everyone and do you think I would ever get a 'Hey, Myron, come up and enjoy the party'? Never. But it's the fate of resented genius—always bridesmaidens, never brides."

Pandy looked at the spot where she'd put her pouch; it was gone. Tensing, she searched the back of the cave with her eyes. Nothing.

"Where's our stuff?" Alcie whispered.

"Excuse me," Pandy blurted out to Chiron and

Myron. "I am sorry to bother you, but we put our things down here before we went to the palace. Do you happen to know where they are?"

"Nope," Chiron said.

"There was some stuff that smelled like horse poop," Myron said.

"That's me!" Chiron yelled. He laughed loudly once, then sighed and put his head in his hands.

Myron just looked at him for a long moment, then turned back to Pandy and Alcie.

"I thought it was trash. It's probably in one of the sacks outside."

"Figs, figs, figs," Alcie muttered as they ran. Pandy beat Alcie to the entrance of the cave and out to the first cart. She caught one of the clean-up servants by the arm.

"Hi! Did you, by any chance, pick up two cloaks, a couple of togas, and some pouches by the back of the cave?" she asked, trying to keep her voice calm.

"I don't know," the tired, glassy-eyed youth said.

"One cloak was a dirty white and the other was—," Alcie began.

"It all smelled like horse poop," Pandy said.

"Oh, yeah," the youth said, scowling. "Strong stuff. You could smell it through the bag! It's on one of the carts. Not the first two, that's all palace trash. Farther back. Don't remember which."

Pandy raced onto the top of the third cart, while Alcie took the fourth, sniffing at every bag. At that very moment, drivers began mounting the first two carts, readying to drive their teams away from the site.

"Pandy! Pandy!" Alcie cried, pointing to the lead cart when Pandy looked up. Then Pandy saw a driver with his crop heading toward the cart she was on.

She looked around, her mind in a spin. She knew what she had to do . . . but where would she focus? If she targeted the trees of the forest, the whole mountain might go up; she couldn't target the metal wheel spokes, because the carts would never move afterward. Then she saw it—and it was so obvious.

Pandy focused her power on the topmost sacks of garbage in the first cart, just as the oxen were turning to head back toward the fork and down the mountain. Instantly, the sacks were ablaze; flames were shooting a full meter into the air, and the light wind was carrying the smell of day-old fish eggs and sour boar sauce back toward the waiting drivers.

At once, surprise turned to panic as embers began rising into the trees and all the drivers and nearby servants ran to help put out the flames. The distraction gave Pandy and Alcie time to hurriedly search several more carts. The flames were finally doused, the oxen had been calmed, and Pandy was just climbing onto another cart, when the first cart began moving again.

Pandy was about to torch a different load, when the wind shifted and her nose caught the unmistakable scent she had been searching for. She ran back another two carts, calling to Alcie as she passed. Quickly, they clambered onto one of the last carts, found the sack, and loosed the knotted cord. Digging deep into a mass of half-eaten grape leaves, soggy squash blossoms, rancid lentils, and crusty hummus, Pandy felt the fabric of her cloak, balled up around her old toga . . . then her water-skin . . . then the leather carrying pouch. As she pulled them out, Alcie dove in.

"Beyond gross," Alcie said, retrieving her belongings.

"At least you won't find any meatballs in there," came a voice from the front of the cart. Pandy and Alcie looked up to see Hermes sitting in the driver's seat. When the two girls just stared for a moment, he rolled his eyes.

"Because Aphrodite ate them all," he said, grinning.

Pandy smiled back at him.

"Going someplace?" Hermes asked.

"We are," Pandy replied.

"Me too," he said.

"Same place?"

"Odds are good."

"Can we get a ride?"

"Do you have the fare?"

Pandy wiped the lentils off her hands and dug into the red pouch, handing the large gold coin to Hermes.

"This should cover it," she said. "I think."

"That'll do it," Hermes said, with a wink. "But it's good for four mortals."

"Gods!" Alcie cried. "I'll go get them!"

CHAPTER ELEVEN
Not So Fast

Each time she turned around, there was no one behind her. Yet, as she raced down the palace steps and along the lower walls, Iole was certain she was being followed. At the path that intersected the back wall and led off into the forest, she heard a loud crack of a twig on the ground and whirled again. There was a slight rustling in the shrubbery, but all she saw was a wall of green hues. She hurried faster than she thought her legs would go until she spotted Homer in the twilight just ahead. Slowing her pace a bit, she waved at him until he caught sight of her and waved back.

"They're not here yet?" Iole asked.

"No," he answered. "I'm getting a little worried."

"They're probably just being especially diligent and precise, checking Pandy's things, making sure the box is safe. No reason for consternation. Let's not get agitated."

Then she paused. "Nice short outfit. Are you planning on changing into your old clothes?"

Homer looked down at his too-small serving toga. He picked up his carrying pouch and headed for a small copse of trees a meter away.

"Don't go without me."

"Wouldn't consider it," Iole said.

"And don't look."

"Gods. You're worse than a girl," Iole said jokingly, watching him disappear. "I see you're still wearing your armband."

Behind the trees, Homer quickly donned his old garments, then looked down at his arm and started peeling away the black fabric.

" 'Need something? Just ask!' Like, that is the dumbest thing I can think of," he called to Iole. "Like any of us knew what we were doing. Armbands! You were in the wedding procession and didn't have to wear one of these. Of course you had to slosh through puddles and ice and leaves, but you got off lucky, right? Iole?"

An ox, yoked to a passing garbage cart, snorted loudly and Homer assumed that was the reason he hadn't heard Iole's response.

"Huh? Don't you think, Iole?"

Homer stepped out from behind the trees, the circle of coarse black fabric balled up in his palm. He looked at Iole, completely unprepared to see a fat hand over her mouth, an arm encircling her waist as Iole struggled, a mound of silvery hair towering behind.

"Surprise!" said Echidna, peeking around Iole's head. "You know, I anticipated this of the other two, trying to duck out without cleaning up and paying me my percentage of the tips, but somehow not of you two. Funny, you just can't tell about some people."

She waggled a long switch she was holding in the hand at Iole's waist.

"Oh, if I had a drachma for every silly temp who thought they could get away with something and had to be taught the hard way. Now then, you are all scheduled until midnight, and until midnight you shall stay if I have to flog the living—"

Homer immediately flashed back to the rotting, undead corpse holding Alcie in exactly the same way during their adventure in the Chamber of Despair. Without saying a word, Homer threw the black armband, sending it with the force of an iron shot right into Echidna's nose, catching her off guard. Iole took that moment of surprise to step hard on Echidna's right foot.

"Oh! Aghhh!" Echidna cried, surprised and frightened.

As the tiny ball of a woman jumped up and down in pain, Homer stepped forward and lifted her by the arms high into the air. He carried her, dangling in front of him like a sack of something foul, over to the closest garbage cart and lightly tossed her on top as it began to descend the slope. As the cart disappeared into the darkness, all Homer and Iole could see were two sandals attached to two short, fat legs sticking up into the air.

Iole came and stood by Homer, watching the line of carts move away.

"Thank you, Homer," she said quietly.

"Not a problem."

"You're very . . ."

Iole deliberated coming up with a very large word, or something a little witty and wry. Instead, she thought better of it.

". . . nice to have around."

Homer just smiled. At that moment Alcie came running fast out of the night.

"Hey," she panted. "You guys ready? We're over this way."

"Are we going already?" Iole asked. "Do we know how to use the coin?"

"Yep. All handled," Alcie called over her shoulder as she led the way. "Prepare to get smelly."

Pandy had been sitting on top of an overstuffed sack of garbage for almost two minutes, not wanting to look toward the front of the cart, when she suddenly felt something sharp under her right leg. Then she felt it again under her left leg. She tried repositioning herself, but nothing helped. She slowly began to rise to sit on another sack when Hermes spoke.

"Top sacks are all bones," he said, not looking back at her.

"Oh."

She sat down again.

"Thanks."

"No problem."

She looked at him. Torches were now being lit along the pathway for the cart drivers. In their light, Hermes' profile was nothing short of magnificent. His was not the most rugged face of the Olympians; that belonged to Zeus. Nor was it the most striking; Ares and Hephaestus shared that honor. Hermes' face was, simply put, perfect.

"What?" he said, glancing back for a second.

"What?" she answered.

His mouthed twitched in a smile and then he patted the seat next to him. Immediately, Pandy made her way over sacks of crunchy bones and sat beside the god.

"So," he said after a moment. "I hear you had a talk with future-dad."

"Yeah. Yes," she said, then she felt a pang. "Oh, no . . . did I wreck it? The future? I did, didn't I? Is my dad going to meet my mom? Am I going to be born?"

"Easy, kiddo. Easy. All is well," Hermes said, chuckling. "You didn't ruin anything. Roughly thirteen centuries from now your father will take that final walk down the road to wedded *buh-liss*, and you and your brother will spring forth . . . and we may just have to go through all this again . . . and again. No, all Prometheus said to me was that he had a chat with a nice serving maiden when he was feeling rather low and that someday, if he ever had a daughter, he hoped that she would care enough to comfort someone in distress the way this girl had. Apparently you produced a tray cloth for him to blow his nose or something. He was impressed."

Pandy smiled in the torchlight.

"Then he took off for a moonlit boat ride with one of Thetis's sisters."

"Okaaaay. I *so* didn't need to know that," Pandy mumbled.

"Hey, your father has thirteen hundred years to meet your mother, give or take," Hermes said. "You want him to live like a temple dweller?"

"Kinda," Pandy said softly.

"He can't even take a nice woman out for a glass of goat's milk?" Hermes asked, nudging her slightly in the ribs (which almost sent her off the top of the cart).

"No," Pandy said, laughing at herself.

Just then Alcie, Iole, and Homer ran up.

Iole stopped short. A garbage cart?

"We're just like Echidna," she whispered to Homer, watching Alcie jump up and seat herself on a sack.

"Not in a million moons," he replied, helping Iole onto the cart.

"Ready?" asked Hermes, when he felt the cart lower with Homer's weight.

"Ready," called Alcie from behind.

Hermes clucked to the oxen, handling the reins with precision as the team negotiated the narrow hairpin turn and moved slowly back along the path to the fork. Looking back, Pandy saw Chiron and Myron silhouetted in the light of the cave, dancing in the moonlight to the soft strains of Orpheus's beautiful melodies, which carried through the dark from the palace above.

"Perhaps you want to get a little sleep?" Hermes asked, addressing all of his passengers. "I know it's early yet, but it's been a rough day, and tomorrow promises more of the same."

"I need to talk to my diary first," Pandy said. "Tell it everything that happened today before I forget."

"As if you'll ever forget," Alcie laughed.

"As if any of us will," Iole said.

Pandy withdrew her wolfskin diary from her pouch and carefully unrolled it. She looked at the beautiful wolf head and for a split second was struck by its uniqueness: a gift from Artemis that would record everything she ever said, and was holding within it the entire account of her adventure so far.

"Dear diary," she said into one of its enormous ears. Immediately, the ears perked up and the eyes began to glow.

"Greetings, Pandora," the wolfskin began solemnly. "What is it you wish to tell me . . . and, oh wow! What's that smell?"

"It's garbage," she replied.

"Garbage. Nice," said the skin. "Very nice. I can see you're doing well for yourself."

The diary, Pandy remembered, had also begun offering its own opinions.

"It doesn't smell *that* bad," Alcie said quietly to Iole.

"My nose is more sensitive than yours, Lefty," said the wolf. "And so is my hearing."

"I haven't had two left feet for weeks, you talking rug!"

"Lefty."

"Yeah, yeah, I was standing too close when the box first got opened! But they got changed back and my feet are *fine* now, you dried up piece of . . . !"

"Lefty," the diary whispered.

"Diary! Just be quiet and listen," Pandy ordered as Hermes laughed softly next to her. He guided the cart downhill as Pandy began to recount all the day's events in order, with Iole and Homer filling in gaps during the time when they were all separated.

"Is this all?" the diary said when she paused for a long moment.

"I think so," Pandy said.

"If I may interject," Iole said. "Tell it that Homer and I sent Echidna down the mountain on one of the carts ahead when she tried to delay us and steal our tips."

"Really?" asked Pandy and Alcie at the same time.

"Lovely," said Hermes. "However, though I personally found her offensive, cleanup will be chaos back there without her."

Hermes raised his hand, his index finger pointing straight ahead. He was still for a moment, and Pandy saw his brow furrow as if he was searching for something.

"Got her," he said to himself.

Then he raised his finger and arced his arm back over his head. High above, they all heard a tiny scream as Echidna went sailing through the night, back toward the top of Mount Pelion.

"And that's it," Pandy said to the diary after looking at her friends for a moment.

"Very well, daughter of Prometheus. Sleep well in the arms of Morpheus," the diary said, the glow in its eyes fading. "And bathe when you get a chance."

"Sleep is a superlative idea." Iole yawned as Pandy stowed the diary.

"Agreed," Pandy replied, crawling backward onto the closest sack.

"Sounds good to me," Alcie said, spreading her cloak over her like a blanket. "Okay, okay . . . pears! What's in these sacks? I can't sleep on this!"

"It's bones," Pandy replied.

"Shall I make you all a little more comfortable?" Hermes asked.

"Yes!" said all four in unison.

"All right. It would be against Zeus's wishes I'm certain, but . . . let . . . me . . . think."

Pandy's head was filled with visions of soft cushions and pillows stuffed with swan's down, and thick silk blankets. Suddenly, all the sacks went mushy . . . and a bit damp.

"There," said Hermes.

"I was expecting something in a light cotton," whispered Alcie to Pandy.

"Excuse me, oh Swift-footed Hermes," said Iole, trying to be polite. "What's in them now?"

"Couscous," said Hermes, and everyone caught the tiny laugh in his voice.

"Thank you," said Pandy first, after a pause. Then she kicked Alcie.

"Right . . . uh, thank you!"

"Thank you," Homer and Iole called together.

It was well after midnight when Iole, Alcie, and Homer drifted off, slightly damp and cold. Pandy remained awake a little longer, knowing that the following day was crucial and she needed some sort of plan for approaching Paris and getting the apple away from the goddesses. Finally, coming up with nothing solid or brilliant, she felt her eyelids grow heavy and a darkness envelop her mind, which, thankfully, blocked out Hermes' endless humming of "Gimme Goat!"

CHAPTER TWELVE

It's a Dog's Life

Pandy woke the next morning to the sounds of muffled conversation from the front of the cart. Then her nostrils were filled with a wonderful, salty, buttery scent. Opening her eyes, she saw nothing but clear blue sky and the very tips of tall trees. Raising her head and peering beyond her feet, she saw Homer, still fast asleep at the end of the cart. Alcie, snoring softly, was curled up like a kitten with her head on his stomach.

"It's not that I value one over the other," she heard Iole say behind her. "I would simply like to get Plato and Aristotle in the same room and ask them both a few questions."

Pandy chuckled to herself: Iole. With a brain the size of the Aegean.

"I can arrange that," Hermes said. "But why?"

"Because I would be interested in hearing them

argue certain points of their respective philosophies with and to each other."

How she and Alcie had even become friends with Iole in the first place was a mystery, Pandy mused, watching the treetops waving overhead. What in the known world could Iole possibly have in common with two dummies like her and Alce? It was at moments like this that Pandy understood that Iole was destined for something great. She might even become the first woman philosopher in Greece. Or she might become a politician and change the law to allow a woman to become a philosopher. Of course, she would first have to argue that women should be granted full citizenship, with voting rights. But if anyone could accomplish that, it was Iole. Then Pandy's heart skipped a beat.

One of the chief things that the gods despised in mortals was any sign of arrogance. Athena had turned Arachne into a spider because of her arrogance over her skill in weaving. Narcissus had been turned into a flower in large part because he couldn't stop looking at his beautiful face. And now Iole was going on and on with her ginormous thinker about stuff no normal maiden would know about. All of the hints, clues, and help Hermes had been offering could just as easily stop if he were to become angry. Pandy was about to say something just to alter the conversation, when she heard Hermes laugh softly.

At once, Pandy realized that she had nothing to worry about. If Iole were talking to Zeus or Hera, or even Apollo, they might take offense. But Hermes, the cleverest and the smartest, would be the one immortal who would appreciate and cherish Iole's intelligence. Iole would never outthink Hermes, but she's the only one Pandy knew of who could make him *think*.

"But can you not accept that each was speaking for his own time and his words should be weighed accordingly?" Hermes was asking. "That values and perspectives, perhaps even morals, might have changed, depending upon culture and history and progress?"

"And that one perspective is no wiser than another, factoring in certain—"

"Iole, you're letting that one burn," Hermes interrupted. "Keep flipping."

"Sorry."

Pandy was hit with a whiff of the salty, buttery smell again.

"Mmmm!" she said involuntarily.

"And good morning to you, sleeper," Hermes said, turning around.

"Something on this cart smells tuh-riffic," Alcie said, stretching and sitting up. "And it's not me."

Crawling forward, Pandy and Alcie saw a thin bronze disc, about the size of a large serving plate, floating in the air between Hermes and Iole as the cart moved up a long hill. Eight huge, double-yolked eggs were frying on top as Iole kept flipping them over with two flat sticks.

"Hungry?" Hermes asked.

"So hungry!" Homer cried from the back of the cart.

Seconds later, they were all devouring the eggs and quickly asking for more. Iole was flipping eggs (as Hermes dropped them out of thin air) as fast as she could, but Homer was eating so fast that finally Hermes just loaded the bronze disc with three dozen, perfectly fried, and sent it floating to the middle of the cart.

Feeling the warmth in her stomach, Pandy looked around for the first time. The Phrygian landscape was not so different from Greece. Olive trees, firs . . . in fact, it looked almost exactly the same. The only difference she could see was that they were going up instead of down. She panicked for a moment.

"You have no faith," Hermes said quietly.

She wished he would stop reading her thoughts.

"Give *that* up, missy. I enjoy it too much," he said as Iole turned to look at him, wondering whom he was talking to. The cart hit a large bump in the road, jostling everyone. The fried egg Pandy was just biting into went flopping into her chin.

"This is Mount Ida?" Pandy asked, wiping away yellow yolk with the back of her hand.

"Of course."

"And we've lost . . ."

"Fourteen days," Hermes replied.

Pandy quickly tried to remember how many days the map had read the last time she looked. "106," she thought, but she wanted to be sure. She pulled the blue bowl out of her pouch and stared at the three concentric rings on the outside. When the map wasn't at work with the outside rings spinning into place, telling her where to go, what to capture, and how many days she had left, the symbols were slightly darker and she had to peer at the number. 91.

"91," Hermes said, interrupting her thoughts. "You're down fourteen *full* days."

"Thank you."

"So, pup," Hermes asked brightly, "what's your plan?"

Many years later, when Iole was recounting this part of the adventure to her grandchildren, she would still be unable to say why she tensed up at that very moment. It was not exactly the unusual word the god had used—"pup"—but something in his voice.

"Yeah," Alcie said. "What are we doing whenever we get where we're going? What are you going to say to sheep-boy?"

"A little respect, Alcestis, if you please," Hermes cautioned. "His name is Paris. Yes, he has a bowl of lentil stew where his brain should be. Yes, he is the worst shepherd on the mountain. Yes, he curses and kicks his dogs until they run. And yes, he dresses some of his sheep and certain tall trees as villagers and sings to them in the moonlight, because his people skills are tragic. But, he is still a prince of the Royal House of Troy."

"But," Pandy said, "*he* doesn't know that, does he?"

"Not yet," Iole answered.

"Right," Pandy went on. "The legend says that Paris doesn't find out about the prophecy—that he's going to bring about the Trojan War and the fall of Troy—until Athena tells him today. He thinks he was born to be a shepherd. He doesn't know he's a prince in . . . in . . . oh!"

"Exile," Iole said.

"Sheesh! Thank you. And in fact his father in Troy, King Priam, thinks he's dead! Thinks that the old shepherd who took Paris as a baby actually left him on the mountain to perish as he was instructed, right?"

"Right," said Iole.

"Is his name still Paris?" Alcie asked.

"It is," Hermes answered. "The shepherd that raised the prince never felt any need to change it, seeing as how the child would never be going back to Troy."

"A lot he knows," Alcie retorted.

"So we can't let on to Paris that we know anything that's going to happen," Pandy said. "We have to be casual about it. We just start, like, chatting. And we happen to be hanging around when three goddesses appear."

"Still doesn't answer the question of how you get possession of the golden apple, in front of the most powerful goddesses in the universe, when Aphrodite gives it to Paris for the judging," Iole said.

No one had noticed that Hermes had brought the oxen to a halt.

"We have to get to him first," Pandy said.

"Won't work," Homer said.

"What won't, Homie?" Alcie asked.

"Your plan, Pandy. He's on a mountainside. With sheep. He's probably been up there for days, or weeks. Three maidens and a youth just don't go walking around mountaintops. And he knows everybody from his village. He would be on guard. I know I would be."

"Very good, Homer," Hermes said. "Paris has the general intelligence of a tomato, but he would be suspicious. Now, if you were to try a different approach . . ."

Again, Iole tensed, looking at Hermes out of the corner of her eye.

"He dresses sheep and trees like people," Alcie said. "He might be grateful to have someone human to talk to."

"We don't even know where he is," Pandy said.

"See those peaks?" Hermes pointed to a high crag. "There's a little pasture on the western slope."

"Apricots! I mean, hey, great! You're taking us all the way up there in this?" Alcie said.

"Regretfully, our time together has come to an end. It

is going to be my duty, my unbridled joy, to escort three selfish creatures to that pasture in just about the time it will take all of you to get up there," Hermes said.

"Huh? Us?" Alcie said.

"We couldn't climb that high in a week. We'll never make it in time," Pandy said quietly, looking up.

"I could," Homer said.

"Fleet-footed Hermes," Iole asked. "What did you mean by 'a different approach'?"

"Homer *will* make it in time. You all will," he replied.

"Tangerines, how?" Alcie cried.

"Four legs are swifter than two."

"Wha—?" Pandy said.

"What would a shepherd appreciate most if he saw it coming at him? Especially one with goat cheese for brains who has lost his own pack?" Hermes asked, smiling.

"Pack?" Alcie asked.

"No!" Iole cried.

"You've got it, my fluffy mutt-let!" Hermes said, beaming at Iole. "Paris just might love a visit from a large youth and his pack of herding . . . !"

Pandy didn't see any part of Hermes' body move: not a twitch nor a flick nor a blink. She only knew that, on instinct, she had turned to look at Alcie. One moment she'd glimpsed Alcie's full head of auburn hair, and the next . . .

. . . Alcie was a dog.

Reddish brown and curly haired, with green eyes and a huge, lolling pink tongue. Iole, still sitting in the front and wagging her tail, was now an extremely small brown-eyed dog with a shiny black coat. Both Alcie and Iole were just staring at her. Stunned, Pandy looked down at her own paws, covered in rich brown hair. Suddenly, the delicious scent of fried egg yolk hit her new, long, black-tipped nose, which was far more effective than her original, and without thinking, she inhaled deeply, licking a tiny, errant drop off her furry jaw.

"This is your figgy fault!" Alcie barked to Pandy.

"You were going to do this all along!" Iole yelped at Hermes.

"Watch the tone, scruffy," Hermes said. "And yes, I have been planning this for a bit. You should thank me. And you will . . . later."

"Dogs?" Pandy cried. "This is helping?"

"Much later."

"I'm a dog!" Alcie barked.

She turned to Homer, still very human, and very surprised.

"Homie, I'm a dog! He can't even understand me. Can you understand me, Homer?"

"It's a little rough, but yeah," Homer said, catching the vowel sounds amid the growls.

"Good," Hermes said. "All right, all of you, off and running!"

"Wait!" Pandy said. "Our things! Where's our stuff?"

"Check the neck," Hermes replied.

Sure enough, around their necks hung small pouches securely tied with strong leather bands.

"It's all in there. It will be restored to its original shape and size when you are."

"But our hands!" Pandy howled. "We can't use our hands!"

"As you like to say," Hermes replied, "you'll think of something."

Without warning, all four were standing on the side of the road, watching Hermes flick the oxen with his crop. The cart moved down the road, and they could see it dematerializing into thin air as the wind carried Hermes' voice back to them.

"Run!"

CHAPTER THIRTEEN
Paris

The speed and agility with which her four new legs carried her body over the rocky terrain frightened Pandy at first. Like a rope tossed to someone drowning, Pandy held on to Hermes' last few words that all but assured her she would be returned to her normal human shape. Then, when she passed what certainly had to be their first kilometer almost straight uphill and she realized she wasn't even breathing hard, she began to delight in her new abilities. Stones and sharp rocks that would have hurt or tripped her human feet, even in sandals, were harmless to her padded paws. Steep ledges and large, slippery outcroppings that would have had to be skirted were now leapt over with ease. Suddenly, she was hit with a memory: Dido, running over the road to meet her after one particularly horrible day at the Athena Maiden Middle School. Running like he was being chased, or like he was a crazy dog. She'd thought then that he had sensed her mood: her frustration and her depression, and that he was running so fast to be able to comfort her. Now she realized that while, yes, Dido loved her and wanted Pandy to know that it was unconditional—no matter what kind of day she'd had—he also just loved to run! Four strong legs moving together—this was bliss!

Alcie, standing triumphantly on a large boulder, howled with joy as Pandy jumped up beside her.

"I might wanna stay like this," Alcie said.

"I know!" Pandy said, although Homer, coming up behind them, only heard, "Rye row!"

Then they all three saw Iole even farther up the mountain, sitting on her hind legs.

"You are gallingly and inordinately sluggish!" she yelped at them.

"Oh, you are so dead!" Alcie said, and took off.

Homer had kept pace in the early going, but two-thirds of the way up, he began to falter, pausing too often.

"Hey!" he called to them. "Let's cut it back a little, okay?"

The girls slowed only a bit to allow Homer to stay alongside. Then, after almost an hour of constant running, Pandy finally felt her lungs tighten and her stomach grow sour. The muscles in her legs were starting to cramp and there was a pinch along her rib cage.

As she stood panting on a flat patch of dirt, Alcie came loping up beside her with Iole in her mouth, hanging by the scruff of her tiny neck.

"Miss Big Words got a little tired, didn't she?" Alcie said after she set Iole on the ground.

Iole lay breathing hard, then she raised her head, her black ears flopping at crooked angles, and looked at Alcie.

"Shut up," she said, then put her head back down.

"Aaaaannnnndddd?" Alcie said.

"And thank you," Iole mumbled.

"We have to be close," Pandy barked, looking at Homer as he walked a little farther uphill to a small ridge.

"Close? I think you said close. We're not close," he said between breaths. "We're there."

Pandy padded alongside Homer and gazed down onto a shallow valley and the most beautiful meadow she'd ever seen. It was ringed with trees and had a little stream cutting neatly through the middle. Pandy envisioned the Elysian Fields in Hades and imagined that the spirits of the undead—the good undead—walked and played on grass that was just this shade of green. Only here she saw dozens of tiny, fluffy white balls just standing about, dark heads down, mouths buried in clover.

"Can I lie down in that for about ten years?" Alcie said, joining them.

"Please?" Iole harmonized, dragging herself to the edge.

"Guys," Pandy replied, "Hermes said we would make it up here in just about the time it would take him to get Athena, Hera, and Aphrodite to Paris. We have no time to waste."

"Five minutes," Iole pleaded.

"Homer?"

Homer heard the vowel sounds of his name and stared hard at Pandy.

"Would you carry Iole?"

"Uh . . . yes? Yes. Yes!"

Homer picked up Iole and gently draped her around his neck. With Pandy leading and Alcie slowly bringing up the rear, they walked down the short slope and into the tall grass.

Ever since the last of his dogs had turned tail and run, Paris had taken to sleeping long hours in the middle of the day at the very moments he should have been keeping watch over his flocks. Two of his sheep had been poached in the last week alone and the youth hadn't even noticed. He was dozing, his back slumped against the tallest fir lining the path around the meadow, and dreaming of a dance. As usual, the closest he ever got to dancing in his dreams was the closest he got when he was awake: staring at whirling youths and maidens as he stood off to the side with the other shepherds, who also smelled of . . . sheep. And there were usually only one or two festival dances held by the time he came down off the mountain with whatever remained of his flock and the cold winter months set in, so his chances of ever holding a pretty girl in his arms were slim to none.

When they found him, his arms and legs were twitching slightly as he spun in a circle in his mind. Pandy noted his dark curls and handsome face. Even dressed in humble, dirty shepherd's rags, there was something indeed princely about the youth.

"We're sure that's him, right?" Alcie whined softly to Pandy.

"Look at the trees," Pandy said. "Look at the sheep."

The tall fir, and two other trees close by, had expertly drawn, brilliantly colored faces painted onto the bark. The two sheep they could see, grazing away from the flock on the other side of the road, were dressed in short, tight-fitting tunics. One was wearing a small headband about the ears.

"That's wrong . . . on many levels," Alcie growled low.

"Many. But look at those faces!" Pandy said. "That takes some talent."

"Guys. Girls . . . dogs. Pandy!" Homer said. "Let's go back."

Knowing that Paris might be disoriented and unsettled if he were to wake suddenly with a stranger towering over him, Homer took Pandy and Alcie a good distance back down the road. Homer set Iole on the ground and began whistling and calling to "his dogs" as he ambled again toward the sleeping prince.

As Homer reached Paris, he saw the youth now had his eyes open and was stretching broadly. Suddenly, Homer realized the next moments were entirely in his hands.

"Hello," he said.

Paris just stared at him.

"Hello," he said at last. "You have dogs."

"Uh, yes. Yes, I do. My name is Homer . . . of Crisa."

"Huh. Never heard of it. I'm Paris. This is my mountain and these are my sheep."

"Good-looking flock," Homer said.

"I guess. Where's yours?"

Homer panicked. He had no story. He had herding dogs but no flock . . . and no story. And just then, a tiny section of the *Iliad,* the epic poem of the Trojan War written by his many-times-great-grandfather, popped into his head: a story of the great warrior Achilles rustling a herd of cattle off of Mount Ida. Homer quickly twisted it as it flew out of his mouth.

"I stole some sheep that belonged to Apollo, and my

punishment is to wander these hills with my dogs, who were my sisters . . ."

At this, Pandy, Alcie, and Iole turned to stare at Homer.

". . . never sleeping . . . or drinking . . . or eating . . . anything. Isn't that right, Alcestis?"

Alcie grudgingly barked once.

"How come I've never seen you before?" asked Paris.

"Just happened."

"Rough," Paris said.

"Very."

"So maybe your dogs can get my flock back together?" Paris said hopefully. "If you're not doing anything."

Iole and Alcie both began to growl as Pandy sat quietly, thinking how unsafe it could be to leave Homer alone with Paris, even though she was almost certain Homer would give nothing away.

Suddenly, there was a deafening crack of thunder and a wide white bolt of lightning struck the path several meters away, shaking the ground. Instead of dust and dirt, a fine blue, green, and gold mist sprang from the impact. The sheep close by scattered deeper into the meadow as birds and butterflies took to the air, raining down leaves and twigs.

CHAPTER FOURTEEN
Judgment Day

"Is Apollo following you?" Paris asked, frightened.

"I don't think so," Homer replied.

The mist evaporated, revealing Hermes standing beside a peacock, with a dove perched on one arm and an owl on the other. Slowly, the Messenger God approached the two youths, one startled and one trying to look startled.

"Greetings," Hermes said, not looking at Homer. "I come in search of one called Paris."

"I didn't do anything," Paris blubbered, then pointed to Homer. "*He* took your cattle!"

Hermes paused for a second, his mouth open.

"Yeeeess. First of all, I am not Apollo. I am Hermes. You might have guessed by the winged sandals, among other things. And this youth does not concern me. You do. You are Paris?"

"Yes."

"Then settle yourself and prepare for the task which lies before you," Hermes said. Instantly, a large chair with red cushions appeared, and Paris found himself seated.

"I'll just, like, be over here," Homer said, moving off to the side.

"Yes, you do that. Wait there, with your *sisters,*" Hermes said, glancing at Homer, his eyebrows arched slightly. Pandy, Alcie, and Iole all congregated at Homer's feet.

"You, Paris, have been chosen to judge," Hermes said. "You will deem the fairest of the fairest. The three brightest lights of Olympus will present themselves to you, and you will choose who among them blazes most brilliantly. And to the victor you will present the spoil. Do you understand?"

Paris stared at Hermes.

"Not really," he said at last.

"Right. Let's go at it this way. Three pretty women would like to know which one you think is the most beautiful. You have to tell them. And *that* one gets a prize. All right?"

"Oh, yeah."

"Yeah." Hermes sighed. "Yeah."

As they all watched, the owl and the dove took to the sky, swirling and swooping, each flying more beautifully than the other (except at one moment when the owl tried to peck out the dove's eyes). At the same time, the peacock spread its tail feathers in a stunning fan, each plume large and perfect. In the next moment, the owl and dove plummeted like stones toward the earth and the peacock let out a shrill, raucous call. As the dove and owl were about to hit, the peacock snapped its tail together again. Suddenly, in a flash of silver light, Athena, Aphrodite, and Hera were standing before Paris in all of their radiance . . . and precious little clothing.

Athena was wearing an incredibly short sky-colored tunic, almost transparent, that showed off her long, muscular legs and arms and her flawless, taut ivory skin. She was devoid of any jewelry except a pair of ivory and gold earrings, which dangled low, accentuating her magnificent jawline and aquiline nose. Her hair was piled on top of her head with a single ivory comb. There was no sign of armor or weaponry. Her lips and cheeks were naturally rosy, as if flushed from the heat of battle. She had only darkened her lashes slightly and was refraining from the stern, intellectual furrowing of her brow. In all, she had the appearance of a regal, impossibly tall woman of incomparable beauty.

Hera, on the other hand, was wearing so much jewelry as to be almost blinding. Fingers, toes, ankles, wrists, arms, ears, and neck were covered in gold and gems. She had on a blue tunic, which hung just below the knees to reveal a well-turned calf and was skimpy enough above the waist to give a view of tremendous voluptuousness. Her glorious red hair was high in front, but then gathered at the back to fall long and loose to her waist. Her lips and cheeks were painted a lovely red, and her eyelids were done in muted peacock colors. She was a marvelous, superb vision.

Aphrodite was—there really was no other word for it, Pandy thought—naked. No tunic. No sandals. She wore her enchanted girdle and several long strands of dramatically large pearls, which covered everything that needed to be covered, no matter which way she turned— but just barely. And her hair was long, thick, golden, and free. She wore no makeup. She needed nothing. Perfect pink lips, round cheeks, arched brows, and the most glorious smile.

The same thought was going through everyone's mind: it would have been a daunting choice for anyone.

Pandy looked up at Homer, who was frozen in place, a small goofy grin on his face as he gazed, completely mesmerized. Then she looked at Alcie, also staring at Homer, just as Alcie was lifting her leg over Homer's foot.

"Don't!" Pandy yipped.

"Fine," Alcie yipped back. "But he doesn't look at *me* like that."

The three goddesses slowly approached the dumb-struck shepherd.

"Wow!" said Paris.

"You understand what you are to do?" Athena said, her voice at first severe. Then, when she saw Paris was justifiably intimidated, she purred, "My handsome youth."

"I have to pick the prettiest," Paris answered.

"That's correct, you charming lad," Hera said coyly.

"And whoever you pick gets this," said Aphrodite, placing Eris's golden apple in the palm of his hand, Zeus's enchantment keeping him from feeling the power of Lust. As she turned away, she whipped her hair out and around, and suddenly the air was filled with the faint scent of fresh roses. Athena frowned, inhaled sharply, and exhaled a lavender fragrance that washed over the entire meadow. Then Hera puffed up her cheeks and blew the wonderful scent of grapefruit and bergamot toward Paris. She also accidentally blew his chair over; Hermes righted him instantly.

Paris took in a deep breath, his eyes glazing. His head rolled from side to side as he tried to focus on the three beauties, and he began to shift the golden apple slowly from hand to hand.

"I . . . don't . . . it's hard . . . I . . . can't. . . ."

Athena stepped forward and thrust her shoulders back, her eyes flashing.

"Let me make this terribly easy for you, dear one," she said. "First off, know this. You, Paris, are not of low birth. You, my handsome youth, are a prince and heir to the House of Troy. Why you are tending sheep on a mountainside is a story for another time, one which shall be unfolded to you in every detail . . . let's just say, don't trust your father when you finally meet him.

"But for the moment, let us consider what would best befit a man of royal blood such as yourself, so long denied his birthright. When you choose me, I shall give you wisdom beyond your wildest dreams. Your prowess at the art of war, your skill on the battlefield, your ability to formulate the most ingenious strategies, your acumen against any opponent will be surpassed only by my own. No mortal man will match you. You will lead whatever army you choose on to glorious victories, and you will deal justly and fairly with those you conquer! Your name will be hailed as that of the mightiest warrior the known world has seen, sees, or ever will see!"

"Really?" Paris asked.

"Why would I lie?" Athena replied.

"Cute," said Hera out of the corner of her mouth.

"I thought so," Athena said softly.

Paris looked at Homer.

"I get stuff!" he cried.

Alcie turned to Pandy and rolled her eyes.

"And you're a prince," Hermes said. "You did hear that part, correct?"

"Oh . . . yeah!"

"Yes, well," Hera said with a yawn. "That's very nice if all you wanted to do was kill people."

She sauntered toward Paris, taking his face in her hands.

"However, I will give you something that will let you do anything your *royal* heart desires, including killing people, if that sort of thing suits you, without getting yourself the least little bit dirty!"

"Ohhhh," Paris exclaimed. "No more dirt!" He tossed the golden apple once in a low arc from right hand to left.

"When you choose me, from that moment on, you will indeed take a throne, something your family has for so long denied you. You, Paris, will rule over all the lands of Asia Minor. You alone will have utter dominion over countries, cities, people, monuments, borders, temples, roads, rivers, mountains, valleys, schools, scholars, the arts, artists, marketplaces, market prices, libraries, liberty, agriculture, any culture, inventions, armies, *money,* laws, politics, politicians, who comes, who goes, viaducts, aqueducts, tear ducts, religions, priestesses, philosophers, philosophies, progress, death, and . . ."

"Yes?" Paris cried, sitting up in the chair.

"Yes?" murmured Homer from beside the tree.

"Taxes!"

"No kidding?" Paris asked, now casually tossing the apple into the air.

"Ultimate power shall be yours," Hera cooed, her lips only millimeters from his ear. "Nod your head and thousands shall do your bidding. King, pasha, potentate, emperor, sultan, majesty . . . how do you wish to be known? Smile and the days shall be glorious; frown and all will know your wrath. And, if I may say, it's a big piece of land. You wouldn't be bored."

"We'll take it!" Homer blurted.

"Hey!" Paris shouted. Without warning, he hurled the golden apple at Homer in a mock fury. The goddesses all inadvertently gasped, seeing their prize tossed about like so much hay. As the golden sphere hurtled through space, the noon sun glinted off its surface. Out of nowhere, Pandy had an overwhelming urge . . . but to do *what*, she couldn't quite pinpoint. She only knew that her body jerked slightly as she watched the apple sail overhead. Just as quickly, Homer threw the apple back to Paris.

"Sorry!" Homer said, looking around. "Sorry. Sorry. Like, not here. I'm not here."

He glanced over at Hermes, who was biting his lip and trying not to laugh.

"It's quite an offer," Hera said, turning her back on Paris. "You won't get another one like it."

Paris looked down at his feet, shaking his head listlessly from side to side, a look of abject frustration on his face, the apple clenched in one hand. Suddenly, his eyes went wide and curious as he—and everyone else—looked directly at Aphrodite. His mouth twisted into a strange grin and he tossed the apple again . . . high. Aphrodite stopped twirling the ridiculously large pearls of her necklace and looked up in the silence that followed.

"Oh?" She giggled. "Me? Is it my turn?"

She blushed and Pandy noticed Aphrodite's nail lacquer turning exactly the same shade of lustrous pink as her cheeks.

Paris opened his mouth to speak, but Aphrodite cut him off with a big, girly shrug of her alabaster-hued shoulders.

"Well, first of all, prince, I can't offer you wisdom. I don't really have any to speak of and Theeny has that covered. Second, I can't give you lands or any of those other terribly important things that Hera's offering. I can only give you one thing. You might not think it's much . . ."

Paris's face quickly registered disappointment.

". . . but if—and it's only an 'if,' mind you—if I'm lucky enough to be chosen, I will give you the undying, unyielding, eternal, and complete love . . ."

Paris's face showed that he had no clue as to what would come next.

". . . of the most beautiful mortal woman in the world."

The instant the words left Aphrodite's lips, Paris looked like he'd been smacked by an enormous frying stone. Homer, Pandy, Alcie, and Iole couldn't tell if his tiny mind had gone even more blank or if many thoughts were flooding in. They only saw that he'd been rendered incapable of speech or motion.

Paris, for his part, was thinking of embracing in his arms something other than a tree trunk, which made for incredibly slow dancing. The other offers were really, really . . . great, but he knew he wasn't the sharpest sword in the arsenal. With both Athena's and Hera's gifts, there were so many things he could bungle. He couldn't even keep his sheep in one place, how could he lead men into battle? How could he rule over lands and people? He'd be killed in his sleep within days, for sure. But this new feeling—something that had rushed into his body only a moment ago—this was bliss! There was nothing wrong with this; nothing horrible could come of it. Now he would not merely dream of holding the pretty flaxen-haired daughter of the village vegetable trader, but he would possess the most beautiful woman in the world . . . whoever that was.

"Her name is Helen," Aphrodite purred, reading his thoughts. "And she resides in Sparta."

"And?" said Athena.

"And that's about it," Aphrodite retorted, glaring.

"I hardly think so," said Hera.

"Oh, *that*." Aphrodite gave a little giggle. "All right, for Olympus's sake. This woman happens to be . . . currently . . . involved with someone else."

"She's *married*!" cried Athena.

"To King Menelaus of Sparta," Hera said.

"But that can all be fixed, if you will, by simply handing that apple to me. With it and my skill, she will willingly leave her husband."

"And?" yelled Athena.

Aphrodite pursed her lips.

"And her daughter," she said rather sheepishly.

"A nine-year-old girl," Hera said, seeming to plead with Paris. "Would you do that to a nine-year-old girl?"

"Rough," Homer said involuntarily.

"Hermione," said Athena. "Lovely girl, slightly horse faced, but she gets that from her father. And her mother would simply abandon her!"

"For *you*!" Aphrodite said, suddenly bright again. "She will sail with you back to Troy, where you will be received at the palace with all the royal splendor and honor you so richly deserve."

"Think carefully, mortal," said Athena. "My offer is much safer."

"So is mine, and you get to tax everybody!" said Hera.

Without warning, Paris heard Aphrodite's voice in his mind.

"The most beautiful woman in . . . the . . . *world*."

Suddenly, his eyes rolled into the back of his head, his mouth dropped open, and, leaning back, he bellowed the most raucous laugh any of them had ever heard. *Ever.*

"And won't she be charmed," Aphrodite murmured to herself.

"Done!" he cried.

He drew his arm down, alongside the chair, and with a great sweeping motion tossed the golden apple high into the air toward Aphrodite.

And in that instant, in that split second as the apple flew overhead, glinting in the sunlight, Pandy knew what she had to do. It was what her canine form had instinctively tried to do earlier . . . obviously something for which her breed was particularly adept. And she could see no other way. This was it: this was the moment.

Time seemed to move very slowly as Pandy's eyes followed the spinning orb. While everyone else was startled, gasping at the fact that Paris hadn't actually handed the apple to the Goddess of Love but had, in fact, oh-so-casually lobbed it in her direction . . .

Pandy leapt.

She used every muscle in her hind legs and sprung with only one purpose.

The apple had just crossed the midpoint of its arc

and Aphrodite, astonished that something, even the thing she most desired, was being *thrown* at her, had put her hands up instead of reaching out. Pandy had a clear path to the apple without anyone's fingers in the way. She caught the apple clean in her mouth and, before anyone knew what had happened, she was down on the ground and running fast.

Alcie and Iole took off and were quickly running beside her, no one barking or yelping or saying anything.

"Run," thought Hermes.

"Run!" thought Homer.

"Good catch," thought Paris.

Hermes realized his mistake when Hera turned to stare at him sharply. Inadvertently, he had been caught in the moment, urging Pandy in his heart to complete this portion of her quest. But he knew that the future would be what it would be; he quickly hid his thoughts from Aphrodite and Athena.

Pandy was like an arrow across the meadow, heading back toward the ridge. Alcie was at her side, Iole trying hard to keep up. They ran as if they were on fire.

"Oh, that's cute!" said Aphrodite. "The doggies like shiny things."

"Look, Hera," Athena said. "The dog is stealing Dite's trinket."

"I love dogs," Hera replied.

Aphrodite giggled.

"Alrighty, bring it back, doggie . . . come on, bring it back! Pup! Pup?"

Pandy was more than halfway across the meadow.

Homer watched Aphrodite raise her little finger.

"I didn't want to do this."

With only a few meters to go, the ridge clearly in sight, Aphrodite crooked her little finger inward and the bone in Pandy's left front leg snapped in two. Down she went with a sharp yelp of pain in a rolling ball of tail and legs. Alcie quickly turned back and found Pandy panting in the grass, her leg twisted at a horrible angle.

"Take it!" she growled, and looked at the golden apple, now lying a short distance in the grass. Without a moment's hesitation, or even knowing exactly where she was going, Alcie set her teeth around the apple and took off again.

"Oh, delightful!" said Hera, smiling.

"Are you going to help me?" asked Aphrodite.

"I shouldn't think so."

"Fine."

Alcie hadn't even built up speed and had gotten only slightly more than one meter when Aphrodite blinked her pale eyelids. Suddenly Alcie stopped short and howled, dropping the apple in front of her. She began turning fast in tight circles and when Iole reached her, she had spun herself dizzy.

"Iole? Iole!" she barked, falling onto her side.

"What is it?" Iole whined. "Alce!"

"I can't see! I can't see!"

"Oh, Gods! I'll give it back!"

"No! You've got to take it!"

"Where? Where do I go, Alcie?" Iole barked.

"Anywhere! Just run!"

Iole took up the apple.

"Assistance, Theeny?" asked Aphrodite.

"I suggest you look elsewhere," Athena answered.

"I'll remember that."

Aphrodite, with a hint of regret but more than a little bewildered at the dogs' behavior, tightened all the muscles of Iole's right hind leg into one large spasm of pain and Iole dropped like a stone.

"That is the strangest thing I have ever seen," Aphrodite said. Then she gazed at Homer. "Youth, you have odd dogs."

Homer looked out at the meadow. Having watched his three best friends tortured and felled, he was too stunned and horrified to answer.

Aphrodite crooked her forefinger toward the far end of the meadow and the golden apple began to rise into the air, taking Iole with it. Iole, rigid with pain was still clamping down on it with all her might, dangling a meter in midair.

"Poor thing," Aphrodite said, and exhaled softly.

Iole's jaw relaxed enough that she released the apple and fell to the ground, watching helplessly as the apple floated back across the meadow and into Aphrodite's waiting hands.

"Aaaaaannnndddd . . . thank you very much!" she cried when her fingers finally curled around the golden sphere. "I know it's difficult," she said, turning to Athena and Hera, "but you didn't really think the outcome would be different."

"This isn't over," said Hera.

"Oh, but it is." And Aphrodite began to sing and dance, thrusting her hips out with each last word. "Paris likes me best, *yes*! Chose me as the fair*est*! That's cause I'm a beau-*ty*. You are simply snoo-*ty*!"

"Excuse me," Paris interrupted. "But . . . when do I get the lady?"

"What?" Aphrodite stopped singing. "Oh! Of course! Well . . . we can be off at any time. Shall we go now? Why not? After all, Helen's not doing anything except getting older!"

Paris arose from his chair, which promptly disappeared. As he strode over to Aphrodite, Hera and Athena stepped into his way.

"You've made your decision, youth," Athena said, her voice low and hard. "Now you will see exactly what your consequences are."

"You've allied yourself with one ridiculously silly

goddess," Hera said, the anger in her voice causing it to rise. "But you have earned the eternal enmity of two others. Two who are decidedly more powerful."

"And more clever," said Athena.

"And just plain mean," Hera said.

"Sleep well tonight," Athena cautioned.

"Perhaps the last good sleep you ever get," Hera said.

The next instant the meadow was on fire. The instant after that, there was a full meter of hard ice on the ground, and Pandy was covered with a thick layer of frozen water. A fierce, violent wind blew from the north and the ground shook for several seconds. Before anyone could panic, the wind, ice, Athena, and Hera disappeared in a puff of putrid-smelling black smoke.

"Sore loooosers!" Aphrodite said with a tinkly laugh. "Pay them no attention. After all, I'm on your side and we're off to get the girl. And it's not as if this is the first time a man has stolen the heart of a married woman. I ask you, what could happen?"

At Paris's blank look, Aphrodite grabbed his arm with one hand and raised the apple high with the other.

"Oh, never mind. Hermes, see you later! This was *fun*! We're off!"

And they were gone in a silver flash.

Homer looked at Hermes, his eyes brimming. Hermes read his thoughts.

"No, I can't do anything. Not my enchantments."

"Can you at least turn them back into humans?" Homer managed to whisper.

"Oh! Yes . . . of course," Hermes replied, snapping his fingers. "There."

Homer just stood, staring, shocked and paralyzed by everything he'd just witnessed, knowing Pandy, Alcie, and Iole were lying hurt far out in the meadow.

"Homer?"

He just stared at the god.

"*Go* to them."

And Homer began to run.

CHAPTER FIFTEEN

Decisions, Decisions

When Homer reached Pandy, Hermes was already standing over her. Homer was too concerned to ask why he'd made Homer run and hadn't simply transported both of them at the same time.

Pandy was in agony. The pain in her left arm was excruciating; it was compounded by the fact that the strap of her leather pouch, now restored to its full size, had somehow gotten tangled up and was binding her arm to her side. Homer loosened the strap and gently helped her to sit.

"I'm gonna go get Alcie and Iole."

Pandy, hunched over, nodded weakly.

Homer raced up to Alcie, still on her side and flailing.

"Who's . . . who's that?" she asked, panic in her voice.

"It's me, Alce," Homer said, getting her to her feet. "I've got you. I'm right here."

"Oh, Homie," she said, tears running from her sight-less green eyes. "I can't see." Then her voice dropped to a murmur. "She blinded me."

"We'll fix it," Homer said, lightly kissing her cheek, then holding her close and whispering in her ear. "We'll do whatever we have to."

"The gods don't take back what they do," she sobbed.

"Hermes just did," Homer said softly. "And if he can do it, so can Aphrodite."

At that moment, they heard a moan coming from close to the ridge. Homer looked over and saw Iole try-ing to stand, then crumpling back into a heap.

"Alce, I have to go get Iole. I'll be right back."

"Don't leave me!"

"I'll be right back." Then, for only the second time, he kissed her very softly. "I'll never leave you."

Alcie was so astounded by his words and the kiss . . . the *kiss* . . . that for a moment she forgot she couldn't see. Homer sat her down again and before Alcie could recover enough to say anything, Homer was off again, running to Iole.

"Can you move?" he said.

"Only my upper extremities," Iole hissed, the words coming out choppy as she fought to keep her breathing under control.

"You mean your arms?" Homer asked.

"Yes, Homer. My arms," Iole replied, then she flickered a smile in spite of the pain. "Gods . . . he tries so hard," she thought.

"Hang on," Homer said. Carefully lifting Iole up, he draped her around his neck just as he had done when she was a dog. Walking back to Alcie, he got her on her feet again and gently steered her toward Pandy and Hermes. Almost there, Homer momentarily looked up from the path he was finding for Alcie and she tripped over a large rock. Down she went, her hands keeping her from hitting the ground face-first.

"Oh!" cried Iole.

"Uh!" Pandy blurted out.

"Alcie!" Homer yelled, then quickly set Iole on the ground next to Hermes. When he turned back, Alcie was rising out of the grass.

"LEMONS!" she screeched at the top of her lungs. "Did you not happen to rotten-apple notice that I am tangerine *blind*!"

Unknown to Alcie, however, her back was to everyone as she yelled.

"Alce," Pandy said, suppressing a smile. "We're over here."

Alcie paid no attention.

"One figgy minute you say you won't leave me, and the next you're hurtling me to my death!"

"Follow my voice, Alcie," Iole said, then she broke into a soft giggle.

"Do you want to see me dead? Is that something that floats your barge? Huh? Dating a dead girl?"

"Alcestis," Hermes said, smiling. "Turn around."

"Who's that?" Alcie said, spinning too far and shouting to the right.

"It's Hermes, maiden."

"Oh." Alcie's voice quieted for a moment. Then she plunged right on, marching across the field and waving her hands, widely skirting the group. "Well, can't *you* do something?" she blurted to a large ewe, which was chewing very slowly.

At this, Pandy and Iole burst out laughing.

"What's that? What's that?" Alcie said, turning toward them at last. "Oh . . . oh! . . . that better not be . . . are you? . . . if you guys are laughing at me . . ."

And down she went again, her foot catching in the grass. When Homer reached her and sat her up, Alcie's face was nearly beet red with fury. Then she opened her mouth to speak but instead broke into a huge guffaw. When she actually snorted a few times, Iole and Pandy fell back in the grass, which made the pain of her broken arm shoot all over Pandy's body. Still, they all went on laughing hysterically. Even Homer and Hermes couldn't help themselves.

"Okay," Alcie said, after several minutes. "So . . . why are we laughing?"

"Because when the human spirit is devastated to the point of madness," Iole said, "both mind and body work in concert to bring it back to some sense of normalcy. It's a balancing act, if you will. A tension reliever."

"Because there's nothing else we can do, Alce," Pandy said simply. "The apple is gone. We're hurt. And I think I have . . ."

Pandy's voice became almost inaudible.

". . . have failed the quest."

They were all silent for a while. The only sound was the chewing of the large ewe.

"So, you're giving up?" Hermes finally asked.

Pandy looked at him.

"What, do you suppose, ever happened to the thing that got away, hmm?"

Pandy knew that if Hermes was still talking, not every chance was lost.

"What do you think happened to the *apple*?" he went on.

Immediately, Pandy's curiosity took over.

"Aphrodite used it to win Helen for Paris."

"And after that?" Hermes asked.

"I don't recall any other legend or story of it being used again," Pandy replied. "Iole?"

"Not that I know of," Iole said, shaking her head.

"Me neither," Alcie said quickly.

"Helen certainly didn't keep it," Iole mused.

"That means . . . ?" Hermes asked.

"That means . . . that . . . ," Pandy answered. "Okay, Helen couldn't eat it. So my guess is that she only needed to touch it, right? Somehow, some way, Eris put pure Lust into the apple. That's why it affected the goddesses the way it did. Then Zeus put the enchantment on it, only to be broken when Paris made his judgment. Paris touched it for a moment, but the enchantment was still on it. Then me, then Alcie, and then Iole. Then Aphrodite actually got it in her hands, which was Zeus's condition, but it didn't affect her as much as it would a mortal. But when *Helen* touched it, it all flowed into her. Then when Helen died, pure Lust must have gotten back into the box . . . somehow."

She looked at Hermes.

"I'm not saying no," he said.

"Then it got out again thanks to me and went back into the apple, right? Right. The apple is gold, so it wouldn't spoil. Nowhere in the legend does it say that Helen kept it. So that means . . . that . . . Aphrodite still has it!"

"Gathering dust. Just sitting on her . . . dressing . . . *taaaaaaaaable*!" Hermes sang, bending toward them for emphasis.

"All right!" Pandy exploded.

"Quest back on?" he asked.

"Back on!" Pandy yelled.

"Let's go find Aphrodite!" Alcie said.

"Oh, wait a minute. Wait a minute," Pandy said. "We can't go to her now."

"Why not?" asked Alcie.

"Because I haven't been born. I haven't taken the box to school. All the Evils, except Lust, aren't out yet in this century. She won't know what I'm talking about. She'll think I'm nuts. Just a crazy maiden who wants her apple. She might even recognize me as the dog who stole it in the first place."

She looked at Hermes, who nodded.

"We have to go forward in time. To the future; what is our present."

"Good girl," said Hermes. "Very well, are you all ready?"

"Wait!" Alcie cried. "We're going like this? There is nothing that can be done?"

"I cannot alter any enchantments but my own, Alcestis."

"Pears."

They were all silent for a moment.

"Okay," Alcie said. "Then . . . I guess we go."

"You might be surprised at what time can do," Hermes said.

"We'll see," Alcie said. "Or *not*, in my case. Hah!"

"Homer, your assistance, please," Hermes said. "See to it that all are touching my garment."

"Yes, Messenger."

Homer draped Iole again around his shoulders, then guided Alcie to Hermes as Pandy got up. Everyone took hold of a small bit of Hermes' garment.

"Keep your eyes open this time," Hermes said. "It's interesting!"

"Would if I could," Alcie thought.

Obeying his words, everyone except Alcie took note of the meadow and the trees, the stream running close by.

"Here we go!" said Hermes.

In the very next instant, it was evident that some of the trees had grown much taller while others were dead or dying. The sun had shifted slightly in the sky and the meadow was smaller by almost one-half, the other half now occupied by stones and dirt. The stream was now on a different course; not cutting cleanly down the middle but meandering off to the right.

"What happened?" Alcie asked.

"Same as before," Iole answered. "The landscape changed. Only this time, we got a glimpse."

"Like, so cool," Homer said.

"Once again, a master of vocabulary!" Hermes laughed.

"We're home?" Pandy asked.

"If by that you mean the correct year, then yes," Hermes replied. "You are also still on Mount Ida in Phrygia."

"I think I can walk," Iole said. Indeed she could, but with a pronounced limp in her gait.

Pandy looked down at her left arm, now free of pain and movable but crooked at an odd angle.

"Your arm and leg have healed! Now, if we'd had to go back in time from where we were, of course you wouldn't have any injuries at all, but since we went forward, time healed your wounds! Isn't that super?" Hermes said. "Naturally, without being properly set, the bones and muscles are a little deformed, but you have your limbs back!"

"I'm still blind," Alcie said bitterly.

"But you have three trusted friends to guide you where you need to go!" Hermes said, kicking the grass with his winged sandals. There was a tone in his voice that Pandy recognized as regret, as if he himself didn't quite believe the lightness of his own words.

"All right then, I'm off," he said.

"Wait!" Pandy burst out. "You're just going to leave us here?"

"Until you figure out what's next, it's naptime! This has been quite the day."

And he simply disappeared.

"Can I take a nap too?" Alcie asked.

"No," Pandy replied. "We need to figure out, alpha,

how to get off this mountain fast, and, beta, where to go once we're down."

"We have to get back to Greece. Perhaps there's a way up Olympus," Iole said, hobbling about. "We could ask Aphrodite there."

"No way up Olympus," Homer said.

"We're going to lose a lot of time just getting to Greece," Pandy said.

Alcie quietly began fumbling at her waist, groping for her red-leather coin pouch.

"Gods," she muttered. "Will somebody help me get this open? Apparently, I have also lost the use of my fingers."

"What are you doing?" Pandy said, opening Alcie's pouch.

"Same idea, different day," Alcie replied. "Look at my coins. Gods, now I realize . . . Hermes was dogging me yesterday at the wedding. I thought he just liked the silly soup. But it's like you with Zeus and his big coin, Pandy. Now I realize that Hermes was constantly tipping me with these . . ."

Pandy emptied the coins into her hand.

"You've got a lot of silver, some gold. What's this? You've got a gold one that says Cyprus. And one that says Kythira."

"And you've got another one that says Tarsus," said Iole, looking over Pandy's shoulder.

"Here's Byzantium," Pandy went on. "And Narbo. And Aphrodisias."

"Great Athena. We're supposed to *choose*!" Iole said.

"Oh, *grapes,*" said Alcie.

Pandy hung her head. Zeus still had to make it difficult. Couldn't have made it just a little easier. No way, no how.

"What do they say on the back?" Alcie asked.

"They all have 'two weeks,'" said Pandy.

"We have to make the right choice or we will just be going from one place to another until we find which one is correct," Iole said.

"And we could lose all the time we have left," Pandy said.

"A puzzle!" Iole said, clapping her hands together, startling Pandy and Homer. "I'm excellent at these. Let's use reason and logic! Let's deduce!"

"It's the one that sounds like her name," Alcie said, but she had accidentally turned away from the others, so her words were lost.

Taking the coins from Pandy, Iole limped slowly in a small circle, gesturing with her hands.

"Zeus knows we're heading to see Aphrodite, right?"

"Has to," Pandy said.

"So the place must have something to do with her," Iole said. "Narbo, Tarsus, and Byzantium. What do these have in common?"

"They're all freaky names?" said Alcie.

"They have nothing to do with Aphrodite," Pandy replied.

"Correct! Nothing that I know of, at any rate. So you take these," Iole said, thrusting three coins into Pandy's hand.

"All right, then . . . Cyprus and Kythira both have temples to the goddess, but they also *both* claim to be her birthplace, so they cancel each other out."

She put the coins in Pandy's hand.

"Guys, it's the one that sounds like—," Alcie began.

"Which leaves only this one," Iole said, tossing the remaining coin into the air. "And I happen to know that they are in the middle stages of building a temple to Aphrodite at . . . Aphrodisias!"

"Which is exactly what I said," sighed Alcie.

"You're certain, Iole?" asked Pandy.

"Pandy, in my house, we pay extra for runners with news from around the known world. At least we used to. And it's not just a temple; they're basically building the entire city to honor her. So, yes, I am certain."

"What were you saying, Alce?" asked Pandy.

"Not a thing," she sighed again.

"All right," said Pandy, taking the coin. "Now, how do we use it?"

"Call Hermes," said Iole.

"Swift and Fleet-footed Messenger," Pandy called,

lifting her head up, her face to the heavens. "Most cunning and artful, I call to Hermes!"

Nothing.

"Hermes? We've decided! We know where we need to go now."

Nothing.

"You think he sleeps that soundly when he naps?" asked Iole.

"I have no idea," Pandy said, gazing up at the clouds. "None."

CHAPTER SIXTEEN
On Olympus

Hermes' vast apartment was, by popular immortal opinion, the destination spot of Mount Olympus, and all the beings who either lived on or visited the home of the gods wanted to spend as much time there as possible. He occupied a single, enormous room on the topmost floor of one entire wing, and when he moved in, he'd had the ceiling removed so the sun, stars, clouds, and tall, flowering potted plants were his canopy. He had a small lyre (an instrument he invented) quartet continually playing the au courant tunes, and great gold bowls filled with individual silver cups of ambrosia on ice. He also allowed gambling and other games of chance provided that, if he was playing, he won. Which usually wasn't a problem when anyone else went up against the cleverest of all gods. It was only Athena on whom he once had to use the "hey, look over there!" ruse in order to move a token to the winning spot, and she had retaliated by turning him into a housecat for a week.

But many simply came for a cup of nectar, to pet the roosters and tortoises (his protected animals were allowed free rein), and to gaze at the amazing walls and the floor.

To the right and left as one entered, the walls were covered with poems and hymns to the Messenger, usually given to him framed when he went to speak at various academies. At the other end was a broad terrace from which one could look down onto the clouds covering the steep downhill slopes of Olympus and onto the terraces of other apartments.

One ridiculously long sidewall had written on it many of the things for which Hermes was patron—and every single individual who was blessed by that patronage. Under bold gold lettering spelling out BOUNDARIES was the name of every person who had ever crossed a boundary in his or her life. SHEPHERDS AND COWHERDS were combined because, in comparison with other rosters, their number was few. TRAVELERS also had comparatively few names. The list of ORATORS AND POETS took up hardly any space at all, but there were thousands of ATHLETES. At the far end, however, was a long list of CONSORTS AND CRONES, a huge portion of the wall was taken up by the seemingly endless names of THIEVES, and over half the wall was dedicated solely to LIARS.

The fourth wall was an enormous map, stretched lengthwise, with tiny red footprints indicating every place Hermes had ever been. It was almost completely red.

But the floor was most astonishing and frightening for anyone new to the room. It was as if one were suspended in space. The floor tiles projected a view, from a single angle that changed on a daily basis, of the earth from a high vantage point; essentially a bird's-eye of a section of the planet, as if the bird were flying a different route each day. One day it would be a stretch of Syria, the next a portion of the Greek Islands, and the day after, the coastline of Aquitania or Belgica.

Hermes had returned, not only from Mount Ida, but also from thirteen centuries earlier, and was unusually tired. He shooed the roosters onto the large terrace, sent the musicians away, and gently but firmly ushered out a handful of nymphs who had come to see a glimpse of Britannia as it passed beneath their feet. Removing his winged sandals and hat, he set his Caduceus on its special stand and settled onto his giant sleeping cot in the center of the room. Within seconds his chest was rising and falling rhythmically, indicating, to the intruder who silently stepped into the entryway, that the god was fast asleep. The day was warm and there was no need for any kind of covering, so Hermes, even deep in slumber, was slightly surprised when he felt something fine and filmy settling over him. At that moment, one of his roosters wandered in from the terrace and crowed raucously at the strange figure in the room, someone who rarely visited and when she did, delighted in viciously kicking the roosters out of her way. Hermes woke in alarm.

But he couldn't move.

Not a muscle. Only his eyelids blinked, staring through the gauzy coverlet. Slowly, as she moved over him, Hera's face came into view.

"You know, I haven't liked you ever since you slew Argus as he was watching over Io—that silly girl Zeus was carrying on with and turned into a cow."

"Yes," Hermes replied softly. "I've sensed a distance between us. Terribly sorry about that. So, what can I do for you?"

"You disappeared yesterday," she said softly. "You and those four brats. You disappeared from Mount Pelion right under my very eyes. And you didn't even bother to say good-bye. So what do I do? I search high and low for you all and I find nothing. Then, you just pop back into view on Mount Ida of all places! Poof! I am thrilled to see that Pandora and company are not in very good shape— my, my, blindness, bones knitted together badly . . . lovely, really. But I want to know what happened."

Hermes tried to struggle, but the filmy coverlet was pinning him to the pallet.

"Know what this is?" Hera asked sweetly.

"No, Hera. Why don't you clue me in," he replied, although he had a pretty good idea of exactly what it was.

"This is the adamant net Hephaestus created when he thought Aphrodite just might be having a fling or two . . . or twenty . . . with Ares. This is the one he surprised them with, throwing it over and trapping them for all the gods to see, all of us bearing witness to Aphrodite's . . . shall we say . . . indiscretion? And you know if it held Ares, it's certainly going to hold you . . . runt."

"Won't Hephaestus miss it?"

"As if I give two acolytes what that idiot thinks or does."

"Well, it's a lovely gift. Thanks. But I don't really need it."

"Oh, but it's my pleasure."

"Why me?" Hermes asked.

"I want to know what the five of you have been up to for the last day and a half."

"I'm sure you do."

"Oh, did I forget to tell you about the new special feature I added? If you don't tell me what that conniving maiden and her three friends are doing on Mount Ida and what they have planned, then . . . ."

The adamant coverlet tightened around Hermes' throat, all but cutting off his breathing.

Just then, on the enormous map in front of them,

Mount Ida began to glow, and Pandy's voice could be heard in the room.

"Swift and Fleet-footed Messenger. Most cunning and artful, I call to Hermes!"

"Ohhhh. She needs you, isn't that sweet?" Hera smirked.

"Hermes? We've decided! We know where we need to go now."

Hera relaxed the coverlet around his throat.

"And you are going to tell me exactly *where* that is," she purred.

"When Apollo pulls the sun backward, that's when I'll tell you anything, you wretched—"

The coverlet cinched his throat again, cutting off all air and turning his face purple.

"You know, I had a feeling that you would remain uncooperative to the last. Let's see if this will persuade you."

Instantly there appeared, at the foot of the pallet, a golden sacrificial tripod. Hermes immediately recognized it as being one of Apollo's prized possessions. The God of Truth used it frequently, burning a mysterious blend of herbs in the bowl, to discern the truth of a particularly perplexing matter or to increase his powers of prophecy. Without even so much as a glance in its direction, Hera flung her hand out toward the bowl and at once a thin ribbon of smoke began to rise from the center. Summoning the smoke with her forefinger, Hera floated the ribbon up over Hermes' body, where it hung . . . waiting.

"Yeah, a little smoke . . . big deal," he wheezed. "You forget, cow, that while I may be forced to tell you a truth, I am just cunning enough not to tell you the entire truth."

"I thought that might be your attitude . . . or something equally antagonistic. You think I'm not prepared? Tell me, *errand boy,* what else designates the gifts of prophecy and truth telling?"

Hermes' eyes went wide.

"No," he muttered.

"I've seen you around them . . ."

"Not that."

". . . When Dionysus would accidentally bring them up from a forest revel, one sticking out of his toga, another in his hair. Or when you helped Perseus slay Medusa. Oh, weren't you trying so hard to act very casual, very collected. Not at all afraid. You may have been able to fool the others . . . not me."

"Don't . . . please," Hermes pleaded.

"Too late."

With that, the thin ribbon of sacrificial smoke floated toward Hermes, streaming through the tiny holes in the adamant and becoming two long, thin black snakes, which slithered into Hermes' nostrils, down his throat, and into his stomach as the Messenger God writhed in pain and panic.

"All right, then," Hera said, watching the two tails disappear. "Now, where is Pandora *going*, and what is she going to do once she gets *wherever* that is?"

Completely at the mercy of the snakes, created from Apollo's own prophetic smoke, and which were starting to lick the inside of his stomach, Hermes told everything that he knew: the wedding, the judgment, Lust in the golden apple, and the group's journey (hopefully, if they chose the correct coin) to Aphrodisias and Aphrodite's partially built temple to beg the apple from her.

"Thank you," Hera said when he finished. "Now that wasn't so hard, was it? Very good . . . and I'm off!"

"Hera," Hermes pleaded. "The snakes . . . remove them, I beg of you!"

"Oh, don't worry about them," she scoffed. "You'll get rid of them—eventually. Now, sleep!"

She snapped her fingers and Hermes went out.

"And when you wake in, oh, let's give it ten tiny ticks on the sundial, you will remember none of this . . . only that you have slumbered peacefully," she cooed over him as she folded the large adamant net.

Striding across the floor that showed the Britannia coastline in the early afternoon, Hera, without a backward glance, kicked a rooster that accidentally crossed her path and left the room.

CHAPTER SEVENTEEN

Aphrodisias

"Are you feeling anything?" Iole asked Pandy.

"Nothing," she replied, rolling the Eye of Horus around in her fingers as it hung about her neck. She extended her left arm at its new crooked angle. "Not a thing. You were right, Iole—it doesn't fix immortal enchantments."

"You mean curses," Alcie muttered.

"Okay, this is nuts. I'm tired of waiting," Pandy said, brushing the dirt and grass from her knees and legs. "He's not coming and we have to get going."

"I'm asking you," Iole said, "why do you think he would just leave us? He inasmuch as said that he would be back."

"Then where is he, Iole?" Pandy asked. The three girls sat on the grass as Homer paced back and forth. Pandy looked at Iole.

"I've formally called him. I used official and reverential words. Then I got less reverential and a little cutesy. I even brought my dad into it, saying he probably wouldn't appreciate it if his best friend left his daughter on a mountain. And nothing."

"Maybe he just wants you to say, 'Hey, you with the silly hat!' Try again," Alcie said.

Pandy sighed.

"Swift Messenger, I call to you. Please Hermes . . . blah, blah, blah."

"What's with the blah, blah?" came Hermes' voice from behind them.

Pandy was so startled that she turned too sharply and knocked Alcie over into the grass.

"Thank *you*!" Alcie cried, facedown.

"There you are!" Pandy said, rising. "I mean, I . . . didn't you hear me?"

"Just now, yes. Which is, of course, why I'm here."

"But not before?" Pandy went on.

"Heard you? Calling? No . . . don't think so. I suppose Morpheus must have sent me some tantalizing dreams and I was just too wrapped up. But, here now, rested and refreshed. All is well. So, have you decided?"

"We have to go to Aphrodisias," Pandy said, handing him the coin.

"Indeed you do," Hermes said, palming it and flipping it into the air, where the coin vanished. "Nicely done, group."

Suddenly, Hermes gripped his stomach, bending at the waist.

"Ooh!"

"What's that?" Alcie said, turning toward the sound.

"Hermes?" Pandy asked, taking a step forward. She realized that she had never seen any of the gods vulnerable, physically distressed, or compromised in any way. It was a bit alarming.

"Nothing . . . nothing," Hermes said after a second. "Have no idea what that was . . . probably just a bit of spoiled ambrosia or rancid nectar. Maybe one of those eggs we fried up this morning, eh, Iole?"

Iole just stared.

"At any rate, all gone now," Hermes said. "As are we. Take hold of my garment one last time, if you please."

As they all once again touched the silvery cloth, Hermes straightened.

"Don't blink."

Before any of them could think, the landscape shimmered, then began to speed past, and then they were thrown into pitch-black for several seconds. Almost immediately, with another shimmer that quickly slowed and stopped, the light returned and the world came back into focus.

The meadow and sheep were gone. Before them lay a wide road and brown, scrabble-hard hills on either side. Trees and a few travelers in the distance indicated the direction of the city.

"That was a rush," Homer said.

"Are we there?" Alcie said.

"You are," Hermes replied.

"Is *that* what happens when immortals disappear!" Iole asked rhetorically.

"No," Hermes answered. "We don't experience the darkness. We can see and comprehend the entire journey across any terrain. But it would be too much for your minds to grasp. So I put out the lights."

"How far away are we from Aphrodisias?" Pandy asked.

"A little under five kilometers. A nice walk; you'll be there in plenty of time for evening meal."

"Time," Pandy said. "We lost another fourteen days."

"A full fourteen days. You are currently in your 76th day. Now, I am going to give you a piece of advice. Normally I would tell you not to visit Aphrodite's temple after sunset; she's not a night person, likes to sleep early and her temple priestesses rarely summon her after dark. However, this particular temple is still under construction and as such there won't be much in the way of guards or activity after dark. I'd go then. There aren't any priestesses on staff yet, no one to intercede on your behalf . . . but Aphrodite knows you, and she'll still be keeping an eye on the building."

"Thank you," Pandy said.

"Not to worry," Hermes said, then he grabbed his stomach again. "Ares' blood . . . this is . . . unusual, to say the least. I may have to go see Apollo. It's nice having a doctor in the family. Oh!"

He doubled over in pain.

"Can we help?" Pandy said impulsively.

"You . . . help?" Hermes smiled and grimaced at the same time. "You're cute."

He disappeared.

"All right," Pandy said, gazing down the road. "Let's go."

Homer braced Alcie against him as Pandy took her other side. Homer's left arm was free and ready; he looked around.

"Where's Iole?"

"Right here!" she said, dragging herself off the side of the road. She was leaning on a rough, freshly severed tree branch.

"Walking stick," she said, linking her right arm into Homer's. "Ready."

The four of them began the slow trek toward Aphrodisias.

"Gods," Alcie said. "I can't even see us and I know we're a pitiful sight."

"Less talk," Pandy said, hugging her, "more walk."

A little less than four hours later, as they slowly approached the city proper from the north, Iole was just wrapping up her history of Aphrodisias—a tale that had begun with the Bronze Age.

". . . and because of the marble quarry close by, they established a school of sculpture, and Aphrodisian sculptors are world famous. My father is a collector; we have several portrait busts. Now, there's an agora which lies between the temple and the acropolis . . . which is nothing like ours back in Athens, by the way. Not so large or important. And there's a wonderful theater and probably the best stadium for athletics outside of Greece."

"Tell her to stop," Alcie whispered to Pandy.

"Shhhh," Pandy said.

"I'm going to kick someone's legs . . . hard!"

"We need to know this," Pandy replied. "I think."

"When my ears start bleeding, you will be responsible," Alcie said.

"Now, the city took the name Aphrodisias only a comparatively short time ago. Before that, there seems to have been a smaller temple here dedicated to some sort of Mother Goddess of fertility. Apparently, when Aphrodite heard of this she did a little housecleaning, got rid of the other goddess, and now there's a whole cult dedicated to her. Although, for some reason, they dress her differently in statues than we do back in

Greece. And she's a little more . . . square shaped. Boxy, if you will . . . not as curvy and not quite as . . ."

"Naked?" said Homer.

Alcie stopped in her tracks and just stared in the direction of Homer's voice.

"What?" he said, getting her moving again as Iole went on.

"According to reports, the temple is quite something. Over forty columns."

Then there was silence.

"And?" asked Pandy.

"And what? That's it," Iole replied.

"Sweet nectarines! I was actually praying to go deaf, too!" Alcie cried.

"Quiet, Alce, we're almost to the city. And I think," Pandy said, looking ahead, "that's the temple just over there."

"That's it," Iole said. "Matches the description."

"Impressive," said Homer.

"Describe it to me," Alcie pleaded.

"Hang on a sec," Pandy said, looking at the sun sinking in the west. "We have a bit of daylight left, but I'm starving. Let's find someplace to get a good meal. I am just not interested in dried fruit and flatbread right now and we have tip money enough to buy us a feast. I'll tell you everything I can about the temple over evening meal, okay, Alce?"

"Deal," she answered.

"I'll tell you everything I know, too," Iole said.

Alcie slumped.

"Kill me now."

The sun had just sunk below the horizon and still the main marketplace was crowded, but not only with shoppers. Many groups of men and women, divided by gender, massed in the middle of the agora. Almost immediately, Pandy felt as if she were under a spell. The air was heavy with incense that smoked out of burners hanging underneath the long porticos. Groups of musicians played continuously as perfumes and aromatic oils wafted out of almost every shop, no matter what was actually being sold. Often, as Homer shepherded the girls through the throng, a man would leave his group and join a group of women, and a woman would do the reverse. Several times, Pandy's face or arm was grazed by the lightest touch of a silk scarf or her ears caught the sound of tiny bells on a woman's earrings. Everybody was very attractive and all were rather liberal in their physical contact.

"Is this a dream?" Iole whispered.

"If it is, then we're all having the same one," Pandy replied.

Passing close by a building, Pandy became fascinated by the many beautifully sculpted faces set into the side. She noticed that this was commonplace on almost all of the buildings, and she also noticed the overwhelming number of statues of Aphrodite . . . but not the Aphrodite Pandy knew. Not the voluptuous vision. Not the one who had broken her arm. These statues showed the goddess well covered in matronly clothing, her feet unusually close to each other and, in every case, her arms were out-stretched as if she were constantly giving . . . something. On her head was sculpted a crown, but about her neck, the citizens of Aphrodisias had placed dozens and dozens of necklaces on each statue. Pandy tried to focus, tried to recognize the immortal figures in bas-relief on the overtunic of each statue, but she was suddenly over-come by the music and a desire to dance. Looking at Alcie, she saw that Alcie, too, was moving in time with the music, feeling the overriding rhythm of the market-place. Pandy grabbed Iole's hands and the two spun in a circle. Unresisting, Iole started to laugh as the smells and sounds, the heady atmosphere, took over. Homer was trying to stay mindful of their purpose and goal, but he felt his body involuntarily relax a bit. That's when he spied a dark-haired youth making his way toward Pandy and Iole, shaking a tambour in one hand. Swiftly, Homer stepped into the young man's path and, with a glare that said "back off," began moving the girls through the crowd, which was starting to become a bit unruly.

After Homer asked directions, they were pointed to a small, fairly crowded tavern named the Singing Artichoke at the far end of the agora. Homer settled Alcie onto a chair at a tiny table for four. A serving girl approached and began to hand out sheets of papyrus stretched over thick boards. On them, in a strange but perfectly readable language, was written the names of all sorts of delicious items that could be ordered for the evening meal: lentils cooked in saffron, bitter bulb salad with honey and sesame seeds, fried leeks with garlic, flatbread with truffle paste, and ("New item!" the menu read) chocolate cake with mint.

"I never thought I would be glad we drank a loony adviser guy in Egypt," Homer said, referencing the ashes of the wicked Calchas and everyone's ability to now perfectly grasp any and all languages, "but it, like, makes traveling a whole lot easier."

"Gods . . . I don't know what to choose!" said Iole, reading aloud for Alcie to hear.

"Let's order everything!" Pandy countered.

"Works for me," Alcie said.

As the heaping platters were set before them, Pandy quickly dished up a plate of bulbs, lentils, and leeks for Alcie, then one for herself. Just as everyone was about to take their first bite, the serving girl approached the table.

"If I may speak freely, sir," said the girl. "You have three lovely wives. A tad young, maybe. Perhaps a little worse for wear, but lovely."

"Figs!" said Alcie.

"They're not my wives," Homer said, answering the girl in her own tongue.

"We're not his wives," Iole said on top of him.

"Consorts?"

"No!" Pandy said, a little too loudly.

"Playthings?" said the girl innocently.

"That's it!" said Alcie, almost falling out of her chair as she rose and turned in the direction of the girl's voice, clutching the table to steady herself.

"Alcie, sit down," said Pandy, pulling her back into her seat. "No, nothing like that. We're all just . . . friends."

"Oh, yes," said the girl with a wink at Homer. "Absolutely."

"Excuse me, eyes *here*, please!" said Pandy, echoing something her father used to say years ago when he was really trying to get Pandy's attention. "I don't know why I should tell you, as it truly is none of your business. But we are all just friends."

"Oh," said the girl with a sudden shock when she realized Pandy was telling the truth. "Oh, I'm sorry.

Then you shouldn't be eating . . . oh, big mistake. My mistake. Sorry."

She frantically waved a young clearing boy over to the table. In a flash, the succulent dishes were gone. She even took a bitter bulb out of Alcie's mouth just as Alcie was about to bite.

She then hurried over to a low side table and retrieved four different menus listing completely different items.

"I'll just give you these to look over instead. Be back in a moment."

"Cold marinated tuna," Pandy read. "Fish of the day with coriander, boiled lamb, fruit salad with no honey, rice and parsley salad, oatie cakes with cream."

"The other one sounded better for some reason," Alcie said.

"I have no doubt," Iole said dryly, now snapped out of her reverie. "We were about to consume a complete meal made from almost all known aphrodisiacs."

"Aphrowhosiwhats?" said Alcie.

"Plainly put," Iole answered, "foods of romance."

After a brief pause during which Homer stared at the floor and Pandy and Iole stared at the ceiling, Alcie finally spoke up.

"So then, this is, like, a wacko cult, right?"

Pandy burst out laughing first, followed quickly by Iole and Alcie. Homer kept his eyes on the floor until Pandy noticed that his shoulders were jiggling up and down as he tried to keep silent, then he burst out with a guffaw that startled everyone. And Alcie nearly fell out of her chair . . . again. Quieting themselves, they ordered fish, lamb, rice, and four glasses of grape juice.

"One large plate of steamed vegetables, please," requested Iole. "Cook's selection. Thank you."

As they were eating, Pandy putting bite-sized pieces of lamb and mouthfuls of fish onto Alcie's plate, Pandy and Iole described the Temple of Aphrodite as best they could. Even though they were not consuming the most appetizing foods, even with their injuries and almost complete exhaustion, without warning Pandy had a momentary feeling of joy and calm. They were so close to capturing Lust . . . the source of it, now residing in Aphrodite's golden apple. Hermes would have told Aphrodite of their need, and she would help them, Pandy was certain. It was only a matter of hours now and another evil would be in the box; that would make four, and they would be over the hump. She felt like rejoicing, as if any and everything were somehow possible.

"Why are you grinning?" Iole asked her through a mouthful of eggplant.

Pandy told them all the thoughts that were running through her head.

"Alcie," she concluded, "I feel that, once Aphrodite knows exactly what happened and why, she'll restore your sight. I feel it!"

Without saying a word, Alcie reached out for Pandy and squeezed her hand.

Leaving the tavern well fed, Homer led them back through the agora and its slowly thinning crowds, beyond the glow of the hanging oil lamps and around the side of the enormous temple. Finding a spot behind a thicket of bushes, without too many rocks on the ground, they sat down. Keeping their voices low and their eyes open for guards, they discussed anything that might possibly happen once they got inside . . . and they waited.

CHAPTER EIGHTEEN
The Temple of Aphrodite

Pandy jerked her head as she awoke with a start. Her cheek was hot and slightly sore from where she'd been pressing it into Homer's shoulder.

"Wha . . . ?" she mumbled. "What time is it?"

"I think it's just after midnight," Iole whispered.

"Why did you let me sleep?"

"Because you were mumbling about Tiresias the Younger and we all wanted to listen," Alcie said softly.

"Kidding," she said after a long pause.

"We had to stay here. There were people wandering back and forth for the last couple of hours, but now they just seem to be gathered at the far end of the agora. This town doesn't close down after sunset," Homer said. "Besides, the temple has been dark inside."

"We have been trying to figure the best way to get some light in there without being obtrusive," Iole said. "But just before you woke up, a lamp was lit."

"I see it," Pandy said, looking between the columns and the unfinished side walls, at a single flame burning deep in the recesses of the building. "It's far enough back that it might be close to the altar."

As she spoke, another flame flared up, then settled into a steady glow.

"I don't like this," Iole said. "There shouldn't be anyone in there."

There was a pause. Then, like a bolt, the answer came to Pandy.

"That's not just anyone," she whispered, her excitement causing her to overpronounce her words. "It's someone who is expecting visitors! Guys, there's only one person who knows we're coming. Well, there's two actually . . . maybe three . . . but the only one who matters is lighting the way for us. It's Aphrodite!"

"You think?" Homer said.

"Absolutely," Pandy said. "She's waited until no one was around and the way was clear. She's lit lamps so we won't kill ourselves. This is a good sign."

"Okay, let's go," Alcie said. "Homie, help me up."

When no one moved, Alcie sighed.

"I'm sorry. *Please*?"

"Alce," Pandy said quietly, "I think you should stay here."

"I concur," Iole said.

"Me too," Homer said.

"First of all . . . Iole? Shut up," Alcie said, trying to keep her voice low. "Homie, I can't even deal with you. And Pandy? Two words: as if!"

"Alcie, we will come back for you as soon as we get Lust," Pandy said. "But it's going to be difficult to lead you. . . ."

"Figs! Figs! I'm coming and that's it!"

Alcie rose and took one giant step toward the temple and stumbled, rolling nearly a meter in the dirt.

"I'll keep going!" she threatened, lying on her back, no longer trying to keep her voice soft.

"Okay!" Pandy said. "Okay. But stay close."

"Oh, yes," Alcie snickered. "I really have a choice."

Getting Alcie to her feet, the four of them crossed the road alongside the temple and, keeping to the shadows, made their way to a large gap in the unfinished wall. Getting Alcie over marble blocks and around columns was slowing them down considerably until Homer simple hoisted her onto his back.

"Am I too heavy, Homie?"

"Don't be silly," he said.

"See, Iole? No trouble at all. *Thppppppth*."

She stuck her tongue out and fluttered it at Iole.

"Over here."

"Oh," said Alcie whipping her head. *"Thppppppth."*

Pandy led the way, around a maze of construction materials and half-finished columns, into the temple proper, guided only by the two small lamps at the far end. At last she found the center aisle, still strewn with debris and bits of scaffolding. Looking toward the altar, she could just discern a large statue of Aphrodite with a platform set in front. Grabbing Iole's hand with her crooked arm, she started forward, and then stopped abruptly.

By themselves, two more lamp wicks flared up out of the darkness. Then two more after that. Then another two. In seconds, every one of the twenty or so lamps close to the altar was ablaze.

Then, as they watched in silence, a solitary figure began to materialize in the center of the platform.

"What's happ—?" Alcie began.

Homer squeezed her kneecaps twice to quiet her.

Pandy was breathing hard, and yet, somewhere deep inside, she was calm at the same time. Aphrodite, in her glory, was by now almost fully formed and was beaming at them all. Her enchanted girdle had been left back on Mount Olympus, and her golden hair flowed down over a simple night-robe. Her skin seemed even more lustrous than Pandy remembered; her teeth were whiter, and her cheeks and lips a deeper shade of pink. The last time Pandy had seen the goddess had been that afternoon (only thirteen centuries earlier) when she'd won the golden apple. And before that, it had been over three moons ago, as Pandy stood in front of all the gods at the end of Zeus's teardrop table and took on her quest.

But now Aphrodite was smiling beautifully at her. Hermes had told her, obviously, what was at stake, and here she was, ready to help. Without warning, Aphrodite stretched out her arms to beckon them forward.

Pandy, Iole, and Homer nearly ran to the altar. Pandy and Iole immediately fell to their knees (Iole winced as her leg throbbed in the new position), heads bowed, as Homer lowered Alcie to the ground.

"Where are you going?" she asked loudly as she felt him fall away from her. He stood again and looked sheepishly toward the Goddess of Love.

"You're in front of Aphrodite," he whispered in Alcie's ear.

"Oh. Oh!" she cried, and clutched at his shoulder as she knelt with him.

At this Aphrodite giggled with amusement and . . . "*There it was,*" Pandy thought. The same tinkly laugh that made Pandy instantly happy, made her think of everything good and lovely. Pandy noted that at this moment, it didn't make her feel that way quite as *much* as it had before, but she attributed that to extreme nervousness.

"Oh, my. So serious, all of you. Pandora, stand now," the goddess said, motioning with her beautiful white hands.

Quickly, Pandy got to her feet.

"Pandora, dearest," Aphrodite began, smiling. "I know why you've come; Hermes has told me everything. You know, I was recollecting that day, so long ago now, with that silly shepherd. Of course, even though you all were there the second time around, so to speak, you didn't really change anything and it all played out exactly as it should. But I had no idea that I had the pure source of Lust sitting on my dressing table for the last three months! Why, I haven't even touched the thing in decades. I mean, really, who knew?" She laughed and tipped her head forward. "We have been watching you, you know . . . oh, I'm certain you must have guessed that by now. And you are doing so . . . so . . . well in this quest."

Aphrodite's voice trailed off slightly as she gazed at Pandy for so long that Pandy wasn't sure whether she should speak or not.

Suddenly, Aphrodite refocused her attention with a tiny shake of her head. With a tremendous flourish, Aphrodite raised her arms high and cupped her hands. There was a golden flash around her fingers and, when she brought her hands down again, Pandy beheld the golden apple in her palm. In that instant, Aphrodite became Pandy's absolute, all-time favorite goddess, and Pandy promised herself that if she actually made it back home to Athens, she would keep a small statue of Aphrodite in her room.

"You have no idea the great joy it gives me to now be of service to you," she said. "I willingly give this token, this symbol, this . . . apple . . . for your cause."

She slowly stretched her long, smooth arm and held the golden orb out to Pandy. Immediately, Pandy sighed with relief and walked toward Aphrodite and her luminous smile. She stepped up on a small pile of rubble nearby to be at eye level with the goddess.

But just as Pandy was about to take the apple, the words "thank you" on her lips, Aphrodite closed her fingers around it once again.

"However, we both know the importance of this gift, yes?"

Pandy was so startled at first that she couldn't answer right away. It was almost as if she'd been roughly shaken from a dream. Things had been going so well, and now . . .

"Yes, Goddess," she said, finally.

"And we both know that I should receive something, however small, in return, right? I mean, I know that your quest is basically going to save the world, and all that. La dee da. But this little trinket has prettied up my apartments for eons, and I just want someone to give up something for me. Is that so wrong?"

Pandy was silent. She was trying to wrap her mind around the goddess's logic . . . or lack of it.

"Pandora?" Aphrodite asked.

"Yes," Pandy answered. "I mean no . . . no . . . it's not . . . wrong. I just don't know what I have . . . to give you."

"Oh, Hephaestus's beard! It doesn't have to be *you* specifically. It can be any of you. And I only want one. It's something small."

"What can I—we—give you?"

Aphrodite smiled bigger than Pandy thought was possible.

"Your life."

CHAPTER NINETEEN
The Choice

Pandy staggered back as if she'd been punched, her mind blank.

"What!" Iole blurted out.

Alcie, mouth open but absolutely mute, grabbed handfuls of air as she tried to find Homer. Homer caught her hands and, without thinking, held her head to his chest. Alcie wrestled away and got to her feet.

"No lemon way!" she cried.

Somewhere in her stunned brain, Pandy realized that Alcie's outburst and swearing at a goddess might be of even more danger than what she'd just heard . . . what she couldn't possibly have heard.

"Alcie . . . Alcie!" Pandy said, moving to Alcie and taking her by the shoulders. "Calm down! Just . . . just be quiet!"

"But . . . !"

"Alcie! Stop!"

Alcie closed her mouth but stayed standing, her hand on Homer's head for balance. Pandy turned to face Aphrodite and stepped forward, her mouth dry and her fists clenching and releasing. She was too shocked for tears.

"D-do you . . . do you want some . . . years off of our lives, one of our lives?" she began. "Or do you want control of our lives . . . do you want a slave?" Deep down, she understood what the goddess was saying, but she desperately didn't *want* to understand, so she was stammering, grasping at anything.

"Oh, I am so sorry for the confusion. My mistake," Aphrodite said cheerily. "No, a full life. One of you has to give theirs up and be . . . well, I guess the word would be 'dead.' I think that's said plainly enough."

"But . . . ," Pandy said, her legs beginning to shake and her lower lip beginning to quiver. "Why?"

Aphrodite looked startled and confused in a way that Pandy had only seen when her father told her mother she'd spent too much on clothes. It was a look of utter incomprehension. After a moment, Aphrodite smiled again.

"Because it's what I want."

And Pandy knew that was that. There was no way to get the apple now and no way to complete the quest without it. Her mind bounced from thought to thought like a pigskin ball filled with hot air. She could rush the goddess, but that would mean instant death. There was obviously no use in negotiating. She could summon Hermes, but if this was Aphrodite's decision, there was no way Hermes could dissuade her. And Pandy wouldn't dare beseech Zeus.

"Take me," Homer said suddenly, jolting Pandy.

"Okey-dokey!" Aphrodite said.

"NO!" Pandy and Alcie said at the same time.

"*Wait!* Please!" Pandy yelled, imploring the goddess. "Please wait. Just a moment. We have to discuss this."

"Certainly," Aphrodite said. "Take all the time you need. But not too much."

Pandy walked a short distance down the main aisle and slumped against one of the tall pillars as Iole, with her bad leg, stumbled over a small chunk of marble and Homer guided Alcie. No one spoke for a long time.

"Why is she doing this?" Iole asked. "What purpose does this serve?"

"It doesn't matter," Pandy said.

"But it's illogical," Iole protested.

"It doesn't *matter,* Iole," Pandy went on. "This is one of *those* times. We have all heard stories about the gods' . . . what's the word?"

"Capriciousness? Whimsy? *Insanity*?" Iole answered.

"All of those," Pandy said. "It's moments like this that no one knows why they do what they do. I don't even think they know."

"Waiting!" came Aphrodite's silvery voice from the altar.

"Can we talk her out of it?" Homer said.

"No," Pandy said. "I saw the look on her face. No."

There was another long silence.

"It should be me," Homer said at last. Alcie began to protest, but Homer shushed her. "This wasn't my quest to begin with. I didn't even want to come and I only stayed because . . ."

He looked at Alcie, her head bent toward the floor, her sightless eyes shifting back and forth. He gently reached out and touched her face. She held his hand to her cheek.

"Homer," Pandy said, slowly and softly, fighting her tears. "That's not the only reason you've stayed and we all know it. You are part of this. We've been . . . family . . . for a long time now. And we need your strength. You *know* that, Homer. There're so many things we wouldn't have gotten through without you. Alcie almost drowned, but you knew what to do. Iole couldn't have made it to shore . . . what? . . . two, three days ago. No, we need you. This whole thing is my fault. Always has been. It has to be me."

"No," Iole said.

"Guys . . . ," Alcie murmured.

"Iole," Pandy continued, "I started this, but you can

finish it. You know how to use the net just as well as I do. You know how to read the map. You don't need me."

"Like Hades," Iole said. "It's going to be me."

"Iole, knock it off," Pandy said. "You put something in the box all by yourself only days ago. You don't need me anymore, and I'm going to do this."

"Guys?" Alcie said.

"Pandy," Iole rushed on. "*I'm* the one you don't need. I'm little and frail and my stamina still isn't a match for you all. And now, to make things really difficult, I'm lame. Yes, I'm smart, but you're just as smart, only you don't know it yet. You think of everything one second after I do . . . you always come up with the right answer. You have to stay. Zeus himself entrusted this whole journey to you. It's always been in your hands. You are the leader, Pandy."

"Iole . . ."

"Pandy . . ."

Alcie abruptly put her hands out in front of her. Then she choked back a tremendous sob.

"All of you," she said with so much weight and authority that Pandy and Iole both stopped midsentence. "Just stop."

After a moment, she began to speak.

"I don't want anyone to interrupt me. You know, you guys never let me speak." A small, sad smile of resignation crept over her face. "This is all very, very silly. Pandy, you're not going anywhere. And Iole, you're too important. And Homie . . . Homer, so are you. The only one you don't need is . . . me."

"Alce—"

"Let me *finish*." She shrugged her shoulders and gave a tiny, pathetic laugh. Then she quickly reached into the red leather pouch at her waist and pulled out all the coins. Grabbing for Pandy's hand, Alcie thrust the silver and gold into Pandy's palm.

"Take them," she said.

"Stop it," Pandy began.

"Take them!"

Alcie paused.

"I'm dead weight, Pandy . . . and we all know it. Yes, I'm funny, but I'm not smart. Not like the two of you. I don't think before I talk; I shoot off my mouth and you have to pinch me to keep me from really getting us into trouble. Someone always has to save me or save us from something I've done. I couldn't walk straight for the longest time and that slowed us down . . . and now I'm *blind*. I can't even move without one of you. I don't have any special skills and I'm not particularly strong or very clever. The only thing I am is your best friend, Pandy . . . and you too, Iole. And even in death, I will always be your best friend. Forever. So will you just let me prove it?"

"Alcie, that's ridiculous," Pandy began urgently.

"It's me!" Alcie shouted, instantly on the move, groping her way back out into the center of the aisle.

"No, it's *not*!" Pandy screamed.

"Yes, it is!" Alcie said. "I said it first. We've decided. Take me."

"Oh, goody," said Aphrodite.

Homer tried to pull Alcie to him, but she slapped his hand away so hard that he jerked it back, stung.

Pandy rushed into the aisle and grabbed for Alcie with her good arm, but with amazing speed Alcie felt for Pandy's shoulder and shoved her so hard that Pandy fell backward over an unfinished column base.

"Alcie!" Iole screamed.

"Shut up!" Alcie barked in Iole's direction. Then her face and voice softened. "I have to." She turned her head and shouted again, "It's me! I'm the one. Oh, Gods, I can't see where I'm going."

"Don't worry," came Aphrodite's voice from the altar. "I'll guide you."

Instantly, Alcie was transported to a spot directly in front of Aphrodite. She swayed for a moment, unsupported by anything, and stretched her arms out, mouthing silent prayers in the hope that, whatever was coming, it wouldn't be painful.

It was only then that Pandy saw the long black snake slithering past them, fast, up the main aisle. As they watched, the snake approached Alcie's right ankle, reared back, and opened its mouth wide, exposing long white fangs. Homer tried to run but found he was rooted to his spot. Pandy and Iole, too, were immobilized, kept by Aphrodite from helping Alcie in any way. Pandy tried to yell but found her voice was gone. They watched in horror as, with a speed almost too quick for the human eye, the snake buried its fangs in Alcie's lower leg. She cried out in agony and clawed at the air around her as she fell to her knees. She lay on her stomach for a minute, then she flipped onto her back, her body convulsing in small spasms.

Pandy thought she was going to lose her mind. There was only one other time when she'd felt so helpless, angry, and lost: when she was watching Iole dangling over the white-hot fire in the Temple of Apollo at Delphi. And then, just like now, Pandy knew it should have been her. She should have been the one over that fire, and she should have been the one now to give up her life. Alcie, Iole, and Homer should never have been brought into this in the first place. If she'd only been stronger when they wanted to join her, if she'd turned them away, Alcie would never have been able to make this terrible sacrifice.

Iole was on her knees, weeping soundlessly and hitting the side of the column with her fist. Homer, still powerless, was standing rigid, his chest heaving, his breath coming in short bursts, sounding like an animal wailing with its throat cut.

It was several seconds after Alcie fell, as the snake was leisurely weaving its way back down the aisle and Alcie's convulsions were growing ever smaller and further apart, that any of them found they were able to move. Instantly they were by Alcie's side. Homer cradled her head, brushing her hair, damp with sweat, from her eyes, as Iole laid her own head lightly on Alcie's arm, sobbing inconsolably. Pandy held Alcie's hand, while Alcie's eyes seemed to be focused on something far away. Each breath was labored.

"Alcie," Pandy choked. "You . . . you . . . dummy!"

"See?" she gasped, trying to joke. "That's why it had to be me."

"It *wasn't* supposed to be you. You beat me to it," Pandy said, wiping a little trickle of blood that was starting to seep from Alcie's mouth. "I was a split second too late."

"First time I win," Alcie said, her words growing softer, "and it was this. Go figure."

She tried to laugh, but it just came out as a tragic wheeze.

"Iole?"

"Right here, Alcie."

"Keep her on track."

"I . . . I promise."

"Homie?"

He bent his head and whispered in her ear.

"Here."

"Don't forget me."

Inside, Homer completely lost it, but he closed his eyes and fought to regain his composure.

"As if," he said, and kissed her forehead.

"Pandy?"

"I'm right here."

"Get 'em back. Get 'em all back. You can do it. You're the one . . . Gods, what's the light? There's a light. Pandy, take care of Homer. Iole . . . you take care of them both, okay?"

Her words were starting to slur, and her breath, already so faint, was almost indiscernible.

"I love you, Alcie," Pandy said.

"Love you, Alce," Iole echoed.

"Love you . . . ," Homer whispered.

"Love . . . you . . . ," Alcie murmured, her head rolling to one side in Homer's lap.

Then she was gone.

CHAPTER TWENTY
The Apple

Pandy was shaking so violently that she had trouble standing up. Racked with grief, she turned to face Aphrodite. Pandy's mind couldn't piece it together, couldn't make sense out of what just happened. If it had been Hades, it would have been logical: still terrible, still devastating, but logical that the God of the Underworld would require death. Even if it had been Ares, bloody, fierce, and cruel, she might have understood why he should exact such a terrible tribute. A human life would be a fitting payment to the God of War. But Aphrodite was all about love and beauty and delight. There was no reconciling her desire for death.

Pandy looked into the goddess's smiling face with new horror and curiosity.

Aphrodite held out the golden apple.

"A deal is a deal!" she chirped.

Pandy stepped up onto the rubble and was about to take the apple in her right hand.

"P-Pandy," Iole hiccuped, still crying. "The net."

Pandy had completely forgotten that touching the pure source of Lust could, probably would, infect her. She blindly fumbled in her leather pouch, still in an almost surreal emotional place, at last pulling out the adamant net. Laying it across her right palm, she watched as Aphrodite slowly lowered the apple into her hand.

Suddenly, out of the corner of her eye, Pandy saw a flash of color. Her head turned and she saw the last few centimeters of the murderous snake just as it was disappearing into the darkness. The light from the oil lamps glinted off its body and Pandy saw that the snake wasn't black at all; the scales in the dim light reflected blue . . . and green . . . and gold.

Pandy didn't have time to compute exactly what this meant before she felt something drop into her hand. Turning back, she saw the apple sitting on top of the net.

"There you go," Aphrodite said. "Just for you. Hold it tight now, don't want to let it fall."

As if on command, Pandy's fingers closed the net around the apple. It felt far lighter than a solid gold apple should have been. Involuntarily, her fingers kept squeezing. Aphrodite began to laugh. Pandy stared up at the goddess, whose face had begun to change drastically. The next instant, the apple exploded into dust, crumbling and releasing hundreds of tiny spiders in her palm. Dropping the net and shaking her hand free of the blue, green, and gold spiders, she looked again at Aphrodite and saw that the simple night-sheath was changing into a brilliant blue robe. The golden hair was turning a deep red, and the soft, round mouth was becoming a vicious, malevolent grin.

The façade of Aphrodite was gone, and Hera stood in her place, hands on her hips, her head thrown back, laughing loudly.

"That's right, precious child," Hera said, reading her thoughts. "Me. Only me. All along."

At that moment, there was a huge silver flash off to Pandy's right. Hermes and Aphrodite, the real Aphrodite, with her golden hair and her enchanted girdle, stood surveying the scene. Hermes, clutching in his fist the two small, dead snakes Apollo had pulled from his stomach, was simply and utterly furious. But Aphrodite had a look of abject despair on her face as she gazed at Alcie's body, then at Pandy. Turning toward Hera, Aphrodite's brow furrowed and a look of anger crossed her face the likes of which Pandy had never seen.

In that moment, something in Pandy snapped—shredding any sense of protocol, decorum, or respect.

And with it, some of her sense of self-preservation. All Pandy felt was the most intense anger she'd ever known. Hera had not only deceived her with a clay apple, but her best friend had died a hideous, tortured death for no reason other than that Hera was a spiteful, petty, evil goddess who delighted in seeing Pandy and her friends suffering in pain.

Then, as if the words had actually been spoken out loud, Pandy heard Aphrodite's voice in her head as clear as a temple bell.

"Do it."

At once, she realized that Aphrodite had read her thoughts, knew what she wanted to do, and was—impossibly, incredibly—giving her permission. Since she was in Aphrodite's temple and the goddess herself, the true goddess, was standing right there, Pandy felt she might have some protection. But all of this went through her mind at the same time her right hand was rearing back.

Without thinking of the consequences to herself or her remaining friends, without thinking of the wrath it certainly could and probably would arouse in other immortals, without thinking that this single act would cause her to become a mythical figure in her own right, Pandy stepped forward . . .

. . . and slapped Hera right across the face.

Iole screamed and Homer choked. Hermes snorted,

while Aphrodite remained silent, concentrating on Hera's next movements.

In the two seconds that followed, as she watched Hera, twisted from the force of Pandy's blow, bring a hand up and touch her red, stinging cheek, Pandy did not for a moment contemplate her own death. She didn't wonder what it would be like or how it would happen. And when Hera slowly brought herself again to her full height, time, for Pandy, began to slow down. As Hera's eyes flashed and she slowly raised her arms above her head, Pandy heard the words, "Filthy brat! Now you die!" as if they were being stretched out like a long piece of chewing sap. Out of the corner of her eye, she glimpsed Aphrodite raising her hands to deflect or lessen whatever Hera was going to do and heard her cry, "Not in my temple!"

None of it mattered.

In the next moment, the world became soundless, and Pandy's mind was controlled and focused like a razor-thin shaft of light. She wanted only one thing and she made it happen so fast that none of the immortals had any time at all to read her thoughts.

Before Hera's condemnation of Pandy was fully out of her mouth, Pandy stared at the wife of Zeus, Queen of Heaven, and the most powerful goddess in the pantheon.

And set her on fire.

CHAPTER TWENTY-ONE
A Whole New Level

The flames were everywhere; not quite burning her immortal flesh, but her eyebrows were gone in seconds and her eyelashes sparked with white heat before each one was incinerated, the charred lashes falling into her eyes and making her wince. Hera was at the very center of the conflagration. She wasn't screaming—that was something Hera refused to do under any circumstances; fear was for mortals. But she was gasping in surprise, another emotion that Hera was unused to, just as she was unused to being set alight. Some sections of her beautiful red hair were turning crispy and black, while other hunks of it were igniting and flying away as ash. Her nose hairs were singed to their roots, causing her to sneeze and shriek like a peacock. The putrid smell of burnt hair filled the air between Hera and Pandy.

But it was only when she saw the hem of her robe and the edges of her sleeves ablaze that she actually comprehended that, not only had Pandy done this *to* her, but it was severe, lasting, and it wasn't going out. Hera began to stamp at the bottom of her robe and flail her sleeves wildly. Suddenly, the flames reached her skull as all of her hair burned away and the thin skin around her brain heated up. She began to slap the top of her head.

Hermes walked over to the inferno. He pulled Pandy, nearly catatonic, down off the rubble and casually tossed the two dead snakes into the flames. Without being able to see clearly what they were, Hera batted them away blindly. Then Hermes turned, very slowly, and gazed at Pandy, her eyes clear white, her fists clenched. He sighed a very long sigh.

"Okay, kiddo. Enough."

Pandy didn't move.

Hermes bent down and put his lips to her ear.

"Pandora . . . *stop*!"

Pandy gave a tremendous shudder, so big that Hermes had to steady her by the shoulders to keep her from toppling over. The flames she had created died instantly, but Hera's garments were still on fire and Hera whirled around, fighting to put them out. Pandy closed her eyes and buried her face in Hermes' robes, convulsing with grief.

As she extinguished the small fires on her garments, exterminating Pandy was not Hera's primary concern, and those few moments gave Aphrodite a chance to step forward, placing herself between Hera and everyone else.

When the last flames were out, Hera instantly turned on Pandy, her chest heaving and her arms raised again, and found Aphrodite standing in her way.

"Move!" she commanded.

"I'm sorry," Aphrodite said sweetly to the smoldering, hairless goddess with the blackened robes. "Come again? I didn't quite catch that. Certainly you would not be giving me any orders in my temple, would you?"

"Aphrodite, get out of my way!"

"Why? One little girl a day isn't enough for you?"

Hera balled up her meaty, blackened hands as they were poised over her head.

"You would *protect* her? After what she just did?"

"What are you talking about?" Aphrodite asked, a tone of incredulity in her voice. "Except for the fact that you impersonated me and killed a child, we didn't see anything, did we Hermes?"

"Nope," Hermes replied, his hand on Pandy's head, trying to calm her because she was now shaking ferociously.

"All I see is you having a rather bad hair day," Aphrodite sang out. The sound of Aphrodite's voice, as it always did, made Pandy happy somewhere deep inside. And this time Pandy knew there was no reason at all.

"You know, I could fashion a wig for you," Aphrodite went on. "Would you like that? Borrow some of Demeter's leaves . . . or I could just put a sheep on top of your head?"

Hera, her hands still raised, trained her soot-ringed eyes on Aphrodite.

"Have you forgotten what happened that last time we were on opposite sides? A little thing called the Trojan War? Your side didn't fare so well. You want to put yourself in that place?"

"Oh, by Ares' sword, are you going to try roasting that old chestnut again?" Aphrodite laughed. "First of all, the sides were split pretty evenly on that one, and you had Athena on your side."

Then she took a step forward and waved away the gray wisps rising from Hera's smoking head.

"Let's see if Theeny takes your side this time when I tell her you murdered a helpless blind girl . . . and tricked Pandora, who by the way, Athena thinks could be just as clever as Odysseus when she gets older . . . all while pretending to be me. As if you could have kept up *that* charade for much longer. I'm surprised, Pandora . . ."

Aphrodite turned and lifted Pandy's chin with her finger, smiling down into Pandy's face.

". . . that you didn't see through her ruse. Ah, well."

Hera stretched her arms even higher above her head.

"Aphrodite, so help me, that brat is going to *die this*

instant and I will take you and the errand boy down with her!" Hera screeched.

"Wife!"

Everyone, including Hera, jumped.

Zeus's voice came booming through the temple again, shaking loose stones and construction dust down from the ceiling.

"Wife? My dream? I seek you."

There was a pause. Hera looked about as if seeking the quickest escape.

"You don't answer?" Aphrodite said. "Let me call him for you."

"Stop it!" Hera spat. "I can deal with my husband myself."

"Hera? Pomegranate seed? Ripe-but-gargantuan grape?"

"Here, loved one," she called out loudly. "Aphrodisias."

A white light erupted toward the front of the temple, growing brighter and larger until the entire inside of the temple was visible clear as day. For a second, Pandy's eyes beheld the true enormity of the Aphrodisias temple, and the different but beautiful flourishes on the columns and side walls. And then she saw the enormous figure of the Sky-Lord strolling casually down the main aisle, his silver hair flowing over his broad shoulders, debris and scaffolding flying out of his way as if tossed by unseen hands.

"There you are, my falafel patty," Zeus said, looking around the temple as Pandy, Iole, and Homer knelt in front of him. "I have been scouring the known world for you. I'd like your opinion on a new color option I'm trying out for the clouds at sunrise, and since it is close to dawn and Apollo is nearly done harnessing his steeds, I felt that now would be as good a time as any. . . . Where is your hair?"

"Uh . . . well . . . you see," Hera began.

"Why is your robe singed?" Zeus asked. Then, without taking his eyes off his wife as Hera struggled to find her words, he sidestepped his way over to Alcie's body and pointed down. "And what happened here?"

Pandy held her tongue, as did everyone else. To expose Hera's part in Alcie's death would have meant exposing everyone else's assistance over the past several months. Not only would Zeus learn about Hera's wickedness but also he would discover where and how she'd gotten her information and that would mean a clear picture of how Hermes, Athena, Hephaestus, and all the others had helped.

"She was bitten by a snake, Cloud Gatherer," Pandy said. That much she could say, certainly; it was the truth. She stood, clinging to Hermes' leg, somehow finding the courage to speak when all others were silent.

"It was . . . an accident." Suddenly she realized she'd just lied to Zeus.

"That's right, Father," Hermes said evenly. "She was bitten by a snake."

"Hermes and I were chatting with Hera when we heard Pandora's cries," Aphrodite chimed in. Her tone was so natural and deceitfully honest that Pandy wondered for a moment if love and lying always went hand in hand. "Naturally, if it had been anywhere else, we wouldn't have paid the slightest attention. But they were in *my* temple . . . in a foreign land . . . *screaming* . . . so we arrived to see what was happening, but found the situation hopeless. And Hera backed into several altar lamps at the sight of the snake."

Zeus turned to look at Hermes as Hera deliberately knocked over a standing altar lamp close by.

"Ooops, I did it again!"

As he stared at his son, Zeus shook his head slightly. Hermes couldn't tell if Zeus was disgusted that he would cover for Hera or disappointed that he and Aphrodite hadn't been clever enough to come up with a better lie.

"Must have been quite the blaze to turn you into a walking egg," Zeus said, smiling at his wife's bald head. Then he gazed down at Pandy.

"Greetings, Pandora."

"Mighty Zeus," Pandy replied.

"I am sorry for your friend. Good friends are hard to come by. You must be on constant guard against snakes, of every sort. However, I am glad to see you. I have absolutely no idea how this happened, but I found something of yours on Olympus early this morning. I can only say, he must be quite the climber . . . I don't think there's even a bird alive that can scale its heights, and yet there he was, roaming the halls and apartments, quite lost. While you have lost one friend, I'm sure you'd like to have another back."

Immediately, Pandy heard a joyful bark from the front of the temple. Moving away from Hermes, she all but stumbled off the altar and toward the light. Almost at once she saw a snow-white fur ball flying down the aisle. With Alcie's death, Pandy had been forced to accept that the people and creatures she loved most were going to be taken from her and never returned; that death and loss were going to be as normal a part of her life as marriage and children were to others, and in essence, that there was a deadly price to pay for being close to her. She had all but given up hope of ever running, playing, holding . . . *seeing* . . . him again, but as Dido jumped on her, licking her face and whimpering with delight, she felt the enormous hole in her heart close up—just the tiniest bit.

"And now we must be off," Zeus said, extending his hand to Hera. "Sunrise waits for no one. Usually."

"I shall attend presently, husband," Hera said, smiling demurely.

"You will attend now," Zeus said.

When Hera didn't move instantly, Zeus walked up to her.

"There is nothing else to be done, my giant nesting water hen," he said low and evenly. "There is no other action for you to take here."

Hera gazed at him, then at all the others, her eyes coming to rest on Pandora.

"As you wish, my lord," she said, taking his hand and letting him lead her up the main aisle. As she passed, Pandora noticed that new red hairs were already starting to grow on her head, although her gown remained charred. Hera called out in a voice laced with honey. "I, too, am sorry for your loss, Pandora. And while I rejoice at your reunion with your beloved pet, I know that the loss of a comrade is such a blow. The dynamic has changed, if you will. Now, for all of you, things are on a whole . . . new . . . level. I wish you only the best of luck."

CHAPTER TWENTY-TWO

Aftermath

As the light faded, taking Zeus and Hera with it, Pandy looked at Alcie's body. She watched Dido pad over to it, sniff the air for a moment, then howl loudly. Pandy turned to face Aphrodite and Hermes, looking from one to the other. Then she closed her eyes, slumping where she stood, and sobbed.

"Oh, my dear," Aphrodite said, moving to her. She embraced Pandy, who threw her arms around the goddess and collapsed.

"That's right," Aphrodite said, stroking her head. "Get it all out. Go on. Watch the . . . the runny nose . . . on the girdle. Oh, never mind . . . let it all go. That's a good maiden. All out."

Aphrodite grabbed one sleeve of her night-sheath and stuck it under Pandy's nose.

"Blow."

She held Pandy close again. A few minutes later,

when Pandy had calmed just a bit, Aphrodite spoke in a hushed voice.

"I forget, Pandora, the infinitesimal amount of death you have actually seen in your short lifetime. We, who have seen so much, and caused so much, have become almost immune to the effects of a loss such as this."

"Pandora," Hermes said, when he saw that she was able to focus on him. "You must know that we would have been here to prevent this if we had been able."

"That's right, my dear one," Aphrodite said quickly, looking her straight in the eye. "Hermes had just come from Apollo and was in my apartments, telling me everything. Everything. What you needed and why. Without warning, Hera snuck up and threw that damned net over the both of us and we couldn't move! She walked over to my dressing table, studied the apple for a moment, fashioned an exact replica out of clay right before our eyes, and then left."

"How did you get out?" Pandy asked, wiping her nose.

"Oh . . ." Aphrodite sighed. "I had to call my husband. When Hephaestus arrived, it was long minutes of me explaining that I was not having a tryst with yet another Olympian. And did he really think that *Hermes* would be my choice?"

"You know, I'm right here," Hermes said.

"Oh, I'm sorry," she giggled. "But really!"

"Not *so* far-fetched," he replied, turning away.

"At any rate, after he finally lifted the net, I grabbed the apple and we sped down here," Aphrodite said. "But too late. I am sorry."

"Thank you for trying," Pandy said.

"Pandora," Aphrodite said, "you have to be strong now. Alcie needs to know, as she's walking in the Elysian Fields—"

"Kicking the dead, calling them lemons," Hermes interrupted.

"Whatever! She needs to know that her sacrifice, no matter how deceitfully won, was not in vain. You need courage . . . *and* . . ."

Aphrodite paused.

"You need this."

Nestled in her hand, in a white silk cloth, Aphrodite held out the golden apple—the original. The one Eris had tossed into a wedding centuries earlier; the cause of so much misery.

"Thank you," Pandy said softly.

"My pleasure."

Iole, standing close to the net where it had fallen, picked it up and held it out to Pandy. As their hands touched, the two girls held on to each other tightly for a long moment. Then Pandy withdrew the box from her pouch and gave it to Iole. Draping the net over her palm, she took the apple from Aphrodite and stared at it: TO

THE FAIREST was still as clear as the day it was magically engraved. Then Pandy held the apple close to the box as Iole, with Homer now standing behind her, removed the hairpin and flipped the clasp.

"On three," Pandy said.

"Right," Iole answered.

"One . . . two . . . three!" they counted together, then Iole lifted the lid and Pandy shoved the apple inside. Iole tried to close the lid quickly, but it remained open a few seconds as the bulk of the apple fizzled away. Pandy draped the net around the open lid to prevent anything from trying to escape, until Iole flipped the adamant clasp into place again and secured the hairpin.

"That's quite impressive, if I do say so," Hermes said as Pandy stowed the box in her pouch once again. "Four down, and only three to go!"

"Only?" Iole said as she looked up balefully at Hermes.

But Pandy had already turned away and was moving again to Aphrodite.

"She's in the Elysian Fields?" Pandy asked. "Really?"

"Well, not just yet," Aphrodite said, looking at Alcie's body. "We have to get her there first, don't we? Hermes?"

"I'm on it," he replied. Then he walked over and placed two gold coins on her lips.

"Solid gold," Aphrodite said, smiling. "Charon can send a few of his grandkids to a really *good* academy with those! Do you want to say or do anything else before she goes?"

Pandy looked at Iole and Homer. Iole shook her head and Homer, as if in complete denial, looked away and started whistling low and soft.

"No," Pandy said. "We're good."

"Call your dog," Aphrodite said.

"Dido! C'mere, boy!"

Dido crept away from keeping watch over Alcie's body and trotted toward his mistress. Then, as they watched, Alcie's body began to slowly disappear. When she was almost gone, Homer took a step toward her, then stopped and turned away from the entire scene. Iole grabbed his hand and he squeezed it tightly.

"All is well," Aphrodite said.

"Oh, Gods!" Pandy cried. "Why didn't I think of it!"

She whirled on Aphrodite.

"She's blind! Alcie's still blind. I won't ask for us . . . you can leave us the way we are. But she's blind and . . . and . . . in a new place. Please!"

"Say no more," Aphrodite said. "I think you all have paid enough to have a little recanting come your way."

At once, Pandy's arm and Iole's leg were both restored to normal. As Pandy stretched her arm in a wide arc, she looked questioningly at Aphrodite.

"Don't even ask, or I'll think you don't trust me." Aphrodite smiled. "Of course Alcie can see . . . although it's rather dark in the underworld. She won't see much. Now we must go, and so must you, I think. It's a brand-new day, new adventures for you all."

"Hey, I'd like to see how you do it," Hermes said to Pandy. "Use the map, that is. Apollo says it's rather brilliant, especially for a Hera design."

"Of course," Pandora said. She produced the map and, after letting Hermes study it for a moment, dragged a finger across her eyes and shook two large teardrops into the blue bowl. As the rings began to spin, Hermes clapped his hands in spite of himself. The three concentric rings finally lined up and the brilliant light illuminated the words "Baghdad," "Rage," and "76."

There it was . . . just as Pandy had feared. She only had seventy-six days left.

"Oh, that's just wild!" Hermes said.

"I guess we'd better get moving," Pandy said.

"Baghdad?" Aphrodite said. "That's Asia Minor, I believe. Persia, to be precise. What do they use there . . . to get around, I mean? Hermes?"

"Beasts called camels."

"Hmmmmm . . . interesting," Aphrodite said. "All righty then . . . take good care of yourself, Pandora."

"I will. And thank you. For the apple."

"Silly piece of junk. I'm glad to be rid of it. Hermes?"

"Right behind you. Homer, will you take Pandy

outside? I think there's something waiting for you at the side of the building."

"Should you do that?" Pandy asked without thinking. "Zeus was just here and if he finds out . . ."

"Zeus has Hera by his side at the moment," Aphrodite laughed. "I can guarantee you that his thoughts do not concern us in the slightest. Go now."

As Homer and Pandy walked off between the columns, Hermes beckoned to Iole. For a split second, Iole thought she was in trouble, that she had somehow angered the god.

"I'm not really good with the comforting, nurturing, mothering stuff, the way the women are," he began. "But I just wanted you to know how sorry I am that we didn't arrive sooner."

At that moment, Pandy raced back into the temple, followed by a spitting camel. Then the camel turned around and trotted back out, and Pandy rushed after, calling to Homer that she couldn't possibly mount it by herself.

By the side of the temple, Homer, barely concentrating and still numb with grief, grabbed the camel in one hand, forced it to its knees, and swung Pandy on top.

"Hey, big brain, back here."

"I'm sorry," Iole said, refocusing.

"Look," Hermes continued. "You made such a big

deal of it before . . . and I really don't need it. I hardly ever wear it . . . so here, you can have it."

He slipped the emerald bracelet, Alcie's Maiden Day gift to Iole, onto Iole's wrist.

Iole just stared at it: the beauty, the sparkle, and the flash. It represented everything that Alcie ever was and would always be to her. It was Alcie, in tiny green stones, hanging on her arm. Hermes put his hand very, very gently on Iole's shoulder.

"But you'd rather have her back. I know," he said. "I know."

Iole looked at Hermes and nodded.

"Okay. That was it," he said, now uncomfortable with the depth of Iole's grief.

"Thank you," Iole said at last.

"Right. Let's go get you on a camel."

EPILOGUE

"Hurry, lord!" the spirit was saying. "It's absolute chaos! No one can cross. No one wants to cross. Charon refuses to ferry this one, and the dead are getting a little backed up."

Hades stormed through the Elysian Fields toward the massive gates that led in and out of the underworld. Passing through, he paused to take note of his ferocious three-headed guard dog, Cerberus, usually barking and snapping, now with each head down and trying to cover all six ears with his two paws.

"Where?" was his only question to the throng of onlookers that had poured out of the underworld to see the spectacle.

But no one needed to point; Hades had only to listen for a moment.

"Wormy melons! What gives? I had good figgy money and I have the right to get across!"

Alcie kicked at Charon's boat, sending it drifting into the river Styx until Charon, muttering, extended his long oar and pulled it back. Then she yelled again at the top of her lungs.

"Hey, you old pitted date, don't gimme any tangerine nonsense! This maiden don't play that way. Is anyone listening over there? There were two perfectly good gold coins on my lips and this son of an apple snatches 'em off my face like he's workin' bread dough, and just because I took a little swing at him, he starts giving me attitude! Like I need that! Then he says he doesn't want anyone like me in his pom-OH-granate boat. What does he mean by that? I'm not good enough? Now he's got the money and I can't get across. Can anybody over there hear me? Huh? Hey you plebe-os across the river! Somebody want to do something, before I take this pruny pear's oar and beat him over the head with it?"

Hundreds of lifeless eyes turned as one to stare questioningly at the dark lord.

Hades tilted his head down until his eyes barely peered out from under his brows.

"Oh, no," he said at last. "I don't think so . . ."

He looked at the throng, then back at the wild girl on the opposite shore, braying for entrance into his kingdom.

"No, I really don't think so. Someone, somewhere has made a big, big mistake."

GLOSSARY

Names, pronunciations, and further descriptions of gods, Demigods, other integral immortals, places, objects, and fictional personages appearing within these pages. Definitions derived from three primary sources: Edith Hamilton's *Mythology: Timeless Tales of Gods and Heroes*; Webster's Online Dictionary, which derives many of its definitions from Wikipedia, the free encyclopedia (further sources are also indicated on this Web site); and the author's own brain.

aquiline (AWK-will-inn): curving downward.

Argus (ARE-gus): a giant with 100 eyes; was guardian of the cow Io and was slain by Hermes.

arsenal (ARE-sen-uhl): a structure where arms and ammunition and other military equipment are stored.

Asia Minor (AY-zhuh): archaic name for the peninsula in southwestern Asia that forms the Asian part of Turkey.

bergamot (BURR-ga-mot): small tree with pear-shaped fruit whose oil is used in perfumery and tea making.

cerulean (sear-OO-lee-un): describes a range of colors from deep blue to sky blue through greenish blue. When used as a noun, it means a light shade of blue. However, when used as an adjective it describes a deeper, slightly purplish shade of blue. Go figure.

Charon (CARE-on): the ferryman who brought the souls of the dead across the river Styx to Hades.

citadel (SIT-uh-dell): a stronghold into which people could go for shelter during a battle.

conflagration (con-fluh-GRAY-shun): a very intense and, often, uncontrolled fire.

coriander (COR-ee-ander): an herb, resembling parsley, used as a seasoning or garnish.

couscous (COOS-coos): a sometimes spicy North African pasta made of crushed and steamed semolina or millet.

dais (DAY-iss): a small stage or platform raised above the surrounding level to give focus and prominence to the person on it.

Elysian Fields (el-EE-zhun): a region of the underworld, extremely peaceful and beautiful, where heroes, those who are favored by the gods, and those who led a good life will go when they die.

Eris (EE-riss): Goddess of Discord; sister of Ares.

gorgon, or gorgons (GOR-gons): three sisters (two were immortal) usually described as dragonlike creatures with wings, brass hands (in some accounts), and live snakes for hair. Looking directly upon any of the gorgons would turn the viewer to stone instantly.

kohl (COAL): a type of makeup used by women in Egypt and Arabia to darken the edges of their eyelids.

Mount Ida (EYE-duh): a mountain in northwestern Turkey, southeast of Troy.

Mount Pelion (PELL-ee-on): a mountain at the southeastern part of Thessaly in central Greece. It is the home of Chiron, the famous centaur, and the location of the palace of King Peleus.

naiad (NIGH-ad): a nymph of lakes, springs, rivers, and fountains.

Odysseus (oh-DISS-ee-uhss): a Greek hero and warrior; his ten-year voyage home to Ithaca after the siege of Troy was described in Homer's *Odyssey.*

Orpheus (OR-fee-uss)—a great musician; when his wife Eurydice died, he went to Hades to get her back but failed.

panpipes (PAN-pipes): an ancient wind instrument consisting of several parallel pipes or reeds bound together.

Plato (PLAY-toh): ancient Greek philosopher (428–347 BC), pupil of Socrates, teacher of Aristotle.

quiver (KWI-ver): a case, usually cylindrical, for holding arrows.

Republic (ree-PUB-lick): is perhaps Plato's best-known work and one of his most influential. In it he explains the fundamentals of his political philosophy and his ethics—among other things.

tambour (TAM-bore): a drum, ancestor of the tambourine.

The Odyssey (ODD-ess-eee): Homer's epic poem describing the ten-year journey of Odysseus after the fall of Troy.

trigonon harp (TRIG-oh-non): an ancient three-cornered harp.

tripod (TRY-pod): for sacrificial purposes, this was a gold or bronze basin or bowl supported by three legs, and it had three ears (rings that served as handles).

zenith (ZEE-nith): a high point, directly overhead.

ACKNOWLEDGMENTS

Thanks to Antoinette Spolar-Levine, James Levine, Riley Shapiro, Scott Hennesy, Liz Schonhorst, Susan Kirschbaum, Gracie Kirschbaum, Deb Shapiro, Anna Dalziel, Melanie Cecka, Beth Eller, Katie Fee, Jen Edwards, Simon Lewis, Debby O'Connor, Dominic Friesen.

With much appreciation to Caroline Abbey . . . who hit the ground running.

As always, special thanks and love to Harriet Shapiro, Ph.D., Minnie, Sara, and Rosie.

DONALD AGNELLI

Carolyn Hennesy

is the author of all of Pandora's Mythic Misadventures. As an actress, she can currently be seen on the daytime drama *General Hospital* and the prime-time series *Cougar Town*. In addition to her full-time acting and writing careers, Ms. Hennesy also teaches improvisational comedy, is an avid shopaholic, and studies the flying trapeze. She lives in the Los Angeles area with her fab husband, cool cat, and groovy dog.

www.carolynhennesy.com

In almost pitch-black, Pandy made her way down the stairs, her hands feeling the narrow walls on either side. Soon, she saw a dim light ahead and a glint of light on metal. She headed straight for it, but cautiously.

The dark pathway leveled out, and within moments, Pandy and the others found themselves in a little alcove lit by a tiny lamp in a niche above a golden door with no handle or knob. She stared at it intently. Then she pushed on the door with all her might.

"Homer," Pandy said with a bit of authority.

Homer threw all of his considerable weight against the gleaming metal, using every ounce of his strength. When he couldn't budge the door even a millimeter, Douban joined him and together they strained for several minutes before they fell forward, spent.

"I don't see any way of getting in," Pandy said, now slightly frantic, acutely aware that Alcie was on the other side.

"Nor would you," came a thin, raspy voice from her left. Everyone turned to see a small, old, impossibly thin man clad only in a tattered undergarment. He was sitting cross-legged on a large stone.

"I am the only one who knows the secret of the door," he said. "I am the only one who may open it, besides the jinn to whom the garden belongs. Who are you and why should I let you enter?"

Pandy began to approach him but faltered after her first step as she saw something slither out of a hole in the wall just above the man's head. She stared as a thin black snake disappeared behind the man's shoulder then reappeared as it wrapped around the man's neck and climbed over his head. Then another snake, white this time, caught her eye as it popped its head out of another hole. Pandy looked around, her legs frozen, as she realized that most of the room—the uneven walls, part of the ceiling, and much of the floor—was crawling with hundreds of snakes.

"Guys, stay very still," Pandy said.

"Oh Gods," Iole whispered in a tiny voice, seeing the snakes covering the walls. "Homer, will you—would you?"

Without finishing her question, Iole grabbed the shoulder of Homer's cloak and hoisted herself up his body, until he helped her to sit on his shoulders.

"They're just snakes," Homer said.

"Yes, they are," Iole answered.

"I will ask again," said the old man as a red and brown snake slithered under one arm and across his sunken chest. "Who are you and why do you wish to enter?"

"I am Pandora Atheneus Andromaeche Helena of Athens, and this is Iole—"

"You," said the man, cutting Pandy off and pointing to Douban. "Who are you?"

"I am Douban," said the youth. Then as if the meaning of the words was only just hitting him, he said very slowly, "The physician."

"You lie!" said the man sharply. "I know the physician. He visits frequently. You are not he. You lie."

In unison, all the snakes that Pandy could see turned their heads toward Douban and bared their fangs.

"No," said Douban, far more calmly than Pandy would have expected. "I do not lie. The great Physician, the man you knew, is—was—my father. He is now dead. And I have taken his place."

The snakes closed their mouths and went back to slithering as the man stared at Douban for a long time.

"That saddens me," said the man. "He was the best of men."

Then he looked again at Pandy.

"Why do you wish to enter, Pandora of Greece?"

"My friend is stuck in a tree on the other side. In the garden," she answered.

"She's in a cherry tree," Iole said.

"We only wish to get her down and be on our way," Pandy said.

"My father has instructed us on the enchanted garden and the three rooms of coins," said Douban.

"Then you know you may not touch a single piece," said the man.

Everyone nodded their heads.

"You may enter to find your friend," the man said, turning his filmy eyes back to Pandy. "But only you. And beware, the danger to which you will expose yourself is greater than you imagine. Attacks may come from any side. Many have tried to walk through the rooms of copper, silver, and gold, and they have all met a terrible end I can assure you, for not one of them has ever come back. Except, of course, for your father, young physician. You would all be better to turn back and let your friend stay in the cherry tree."

Pandy huffed at the suggestion. Remembering her power over fire, Pandy squared her shoulders. "I can defend myself if someone tries to attack me. And I'm not interested in any money—just my friend."

The old man smirked.

"So you say. But what if those who would attack you cannot be seen, how will you defend yourself then?"

Pandy had no idea.

"I just will," she said at last.

"Very well, since you will not listen to my advice and turn away, hear this: when the door is opened, you must summon all your courage to find your way into the first room, which will then be lit as bright as day. Pass through the room as quickly as you can and pay no attention to anything you may hear. Anything. And above all, touch nothing. I shall repeat, although it never does any good: do not listen and do not touch. Do you understand?"

"Yes," Pandy replied. If it was just voices, how bad could that be, she mused.

"Then come," said the man, unbending his legs and rising. Pandy noticed that, while the old man had been talking, all the snakes had simply disappeared. Moving swiftly to the golden door, the man gave the gentlest push and it swung silently inward revealing nothing but blackness beyond.

Pandy looked to Iole, Homer, and Douban, her smile weak but her fists clenched firmly. Then she walked into the darkness. Remembering that she had forgotten to ask anything about the garden itself, its size, shape or where exactly to find Alcie, Pandy turned back but the golden door was swinging shut and, suddenly, she was in pitch—pitch—black.

It was then Pandy recalled the words spoken by the head of Douban's father: "the deadly corridor." And she flashed back to the first words of advice the old man had just given her: "You must summon all your courage to find your way into the first room."

Pandy had just assumed that she would be in some sort of rocky passageway, much like the one she and the others had passed through as they descended the stairway into the earth from above. Why would she need any courage? Couldn't she just walk?

It was then, as her eyes were trying to adjust, trying to find even a pinpoint of light to lead her, she heard the sound. So very soft. All around her, a rustling, but not harsh—whisper soft. It was the sound of things gently rubbing together, oh so slowly.

Tentatively, she put out her hand, trying to find a wall with her fingers. Nothing. She edged forward, slowly. Finally, her middle finger brushed against something soft and dry. Pandy pulled her hand back, then stretched it out again cautiously, feeling again the papery softness.

Then she felt it move.

In the blink of an eye, just before she jerked her hand away, she felt the tiny but strong muscles contract. She knew exactly what it was. And she flashed on all the small heads turning toward Douban, fangs bared.

All the snakes that had disappeared from the alcove were now surrounding her; her skin rose up in prickles along the back of her neck and down her arms and legs. She remained frozen for—she couldn't say how long. She hadn't known this particular type of fear before: to be completely unable to see the enemy, to see what was coming at you. Then she remembered that her feet hadn't come into contact with anything so, perhaps, shuffling along the floor wouldn't be dangerous. Her legs felt like they were made of bronze. She forced herself to go onward until her shoulder grazed a wall and she felt a mass of long shapes on her upper arm.

"Okay. Okay," she mouthed to herself. "This is not the way. I could be in here forever, bumping into walls. Think!"

Without knowing why exactly, only that she was, naturally, curious, she gradually raised her right arm into the air over her head. Her elbow was still bent when she brushed against a ceiling writhing with long, slender bodies—so close to her head.

She gritted her teeth and hesitantly put out her hand one more time.

"If I can just move along a wall," she mumbled.

She closed her eyes; there was no point in keeping them open, she knew she could only rely on her fingers and her sense of touch. She lightly traced over a mass of snakes slithering on a wall. Moving forward, she delicately swept her forefinger along one particular snake or another always avoiding the head. This worked until she headed into a corner and her nose rammed between two snakes clinging to wall. Instantly, she flung her head back but not before her cheek felt a tiny fang, bared and ready to strike.

Around and around she went. She lost any sense of time. Into dead-ends, oddly angled corners, and wide, sweeping curves. At one point, the ceiling sloped downward and a hanging tail lightly struck the top of her head. She was beyond tired. She got on her knees, still keeping her arms stretched out, mashing her knees into the hard ground as she willed herself onward.

"Alcie's alive and, by Zeus and all the gods, I'm going to find her," she said aloud, not caring if the snakes were at all disturbed.

Then she felt it.

The air became ever-so-slightly cooler and less stale.

Pandy had an urge to speed up, but resisted with all her might. She kept her pace even, but felt over her head and realized she could stand again. Then, all at once, she felt a bare spot on the wall to her right and her fingers touched only stone. Then more stone as the gaps between snakes grew wider, then she placed her palm on the wall and felt only smoothness. Impulsively, she raised her left arm and felt the ceiling, devoid of snakes.

Suddenly the wall and ceiling ended and she was standing alone in the blackness. She opened her eyes. There was nothing to cling to, no focus point. She began to lose any sense of direction, becoming uncertain of which way was up and which way was down. Just as she began to stumble forward, a light was lit in a room, the opening to which was directly in front of her. Immediately, she stepped into the archway and, steadying herself against a wall, turned to look behind her.

There was nothing. She had seen this kind of blackness only once before, when she'd been sucked into the void of the heavens. She'd seen the great masses that formed the constellations up close, but beyond them, a darkness that went beyond an ordinary moonless night. This corridor or chamber . . . or whatever she'd just passed through had been exactly the same.

Pandy turned back into the long room to find that it was now awash in light. There wasn't a soul in sight, but many oil lamps hanging from the ceiling were now blazing, turning the room red. Pandy realized that the walls and ceiling were covered entirely in copper. Beyond this room another archway led into darkness, but Pandy knew that Alcie was close by. She headed quickly, in a straight line, for the archway, only glancing at the huge jars, close to the walls on either side, full to bursting with red copper coins. She wasn't ten steps into the room when the first voice whispered in her ear.

"Take one—who will know?"

Then another voice in her other ear.

"Aren't they pretty? And you could use them, no?"

Suddenly the voices were all around her. Some were light and airy, others sweet, but all were playful.

"Just a handful." "We won't tell." "Come, over here!" "This way!"

Then, a voice crept in that was anything but sweet.

"Stop her. Stop her before she goes any farther!"

Both Pandy's courage and footsteps faltered for a moment.

"There! You see? She's listening. Tell her! Tell her what we will do to her if she takes another step." "Do not let her pass!" "Take a coin, just one."

Pandy remembered the words of the old man and walked straight across the long room. The tempting words and the threats died out quickly as she reached the entryway to the second room, which was magically lit before her.

"Okay," she murmured to herself, glancing back into the copper room, now completely dark. "Not bad. Not great, but not bad."

She peered into the new room. It was blinding white, covered from top to bottom in silver. Large jars piled high with shiny silver coins lined the walls, and there were many more black stones on the floor around them. She squared her shoulders and walked ahead. Only five steps into the room, however, and the voices were back.

"Where does she think she's going?" "What does she want here?" "Such beautiful coins—take some."

The voices grew in ferocity and temptation.

"Catch her!" "Kill her!" "The coins are enchanted, such powers they would give you!" "The death of a thousand cuts!" "Your eyes will be torn away!" "All of this silver is yours, take it!"

With a start Pandy realized that she had stopped in the middle of the room and was staring at the gleaming piles of coins.

"That's it!" "Take one, ten—take them all!"

She couldn't remember the last time she had seen so much silver. Even the silver merchant in the marketplace had not such a quantity.

"Figs," she said absentmindedly. And that word brought her right back to Alcie. Alcie, only one room and a few measly trees away! She turned her steps toward the entrance to the third room and, reaching it, didn't even bother to look behind her; she knew the silver room was now dark, and if it wasn't, she didn't care. The third and final room lay before her, made entirely of gleaming gold and now ablaze with the light of dozens of oil lamps. So many jars of beautiful golden coins lined the walls, three or four deep in places, that she lost count. She had never in her life seen so much money. She'd seen splendor, to be certain, but never simple, pure golden *money*. There was so much it was even piled in heaps on the floor. And so many black rocks. There were more rounded rocks in this room than in the first two combined.

She took a quick glance around; the only physical difference to this room that she could see was the absence of a far wall. Instead, the room opened onto an expanse of blackness. Then Pandy narrowed her eyes and stared hard. There was a twinkle to the left, then a sparkle to the right, and then a flash, and then another and another, all accompanied by a delicate clinking sound. Finally, her eyes made out the large trees with low-hanging fruit that tinkled and glinted in the lamplight. And far beyond the trees, a single candle or lamp or flame of some sort sputtered in the blackness.

"The garden!" she gasped.

"Hey! I see a light!" came a voice from somewhere deep in the grove of trees.

"Alcie!" yelled Pandy.

"Pandy?" yelled Alcie in return.

Without another word, Pandy broke into a run . . .